BIRDIE TELL ME MORE...

ANJU PRADHAN (SAI PREMA)

Chennai • Bangalore

CLEVER FOX PUBLISHING
Chennai, India

Published by CLEVER FOX PUBLISHING 2024
Copyright © Anju Pradhan (Sai Prema) 2024

All Rights Reserved.
ISBN: 978-93-56487-73-4

This book has been published with all reasonable efforts taken to make the material error-free after the consent of the author. No part of this book shall be used, reproduced in any manner whatsoever without written permission from the author, except in the case of brief quotations embodied in critical articles and reviews.

The Author of this book is solely responsible and liable for its content including but not limited to the views, representations, descriptions, statements, information, opinions and references ["Content"]. The Content of this book shall not constitute or be construed or deemed to reflect the opinion or expression of the Publisher or Editor. Neither the Publisher nor Editor endorse or approve the Content of this book or guarantee the reliability, accuracy or completeness of the Content published herein and do not make any representations or warranties of any kind, express or implied, including but not limited to the implied warranties of merchantability, fitness for a particular purpose. The Publisher and Editor shall not be liable whatsoever for any errors, omissions, whether such errors or omissions result from negligence, accident, or any other cause or claims for loss or damages of any kind, including without limitation, indirect or consequential loss or damage arising out of use, inability to use, or about the reliability, accuracy or sufficiency of the information contained in this book.

"Bessie is my name. I am twelve years old, plump, chubby, and an introvert."

> **"Be simple, be sincere, be sweet."**
> – BHAGWAN SHREE SATHYA SAI BABA

This book is dedicated to the Lotus Feet of Bhagwan Shree Sathya Sai Baba.

The Lord has been my inspiration, guide, and mentor.

It is because of Bhagwan's blessings showered upon me, that I have been able to pen down a few words of encouragement for my readers.

I still remember my beloved mummy, holding my small fingers and forcing me to read my first book "NODDY".

No wonder it is said, "God cannot be everywhere, that's why he created: MOTHER"

ACKNOWLEDGMENT

*M*y 'SUPER-HERO'-DAD-is next to God for me. He never refused to buy books for me. He has been the one to take me to the library regularly since my school days.

For a start, 'What Katy Did' was the book, which he had purchased for me. After that, a variety of books, by different authors, started filling my shelves. My parents gave me the best jewels in my life, which are 'BOOKS'.

How can I forget to thank all my near and dear ones who always supported me when I needed them.

8:30 AM, SATURDAY

Cuckoo! Cuckoo! Chirp! Chirp! Tring! Tring!

Oh! My God! How I detest the twitter of birds early in the morning, and this alarm clock of mine, which hardly lets me sleep.

Tring! Tring! It kept on ringing right inside my ears.

Dear readers, allow me to give you a brief description of myself. I am Bessie. People find me cute (but I doubt it), plump from every corner, and, last but not least…an introvert.

Chirp! Chirp! The birds twittered again with their tiny feet gently perched on a branch of the tree, which is just outside my large pink-colored window.

"Will you guys let me live in peace please?" I screeched at the top of my voice, covering my elf-like ears with a plushie doggie pillow. At that moment, I felt as if my intestines would come out and start dancing on the floor. "One more chirp, then…then…," I mumbled. I got stuck, as even I didn't know what I would have done to them. I hated their twitter, but I wasn't a bird killer.

"If you cannot control the situation, why stress over it", a tiny, crispy voice boomed from somewhere. "What?" I asked myself.

"Am I hearing voices? Or is it just that I am reading too many fantasy novels?"

I looked around the room, wondering where the voice was coming from. I looked under my bed, inside my wardrobe, amidst my books, inside my washroom, can that be Mr. India? A huge 'No'.

"Learn to let it go". Again, the same voice echoed around my room. "Hey!" I called out, mustering my guts. "Whoever you are, why don't you show your face in front of me?" I had never uttered such a long sentence to anyone in my life; this was the first time. I flopped on my bean bag and could feel my heart hammering, my knees turning into jelly. I felt as if a lobster had got stuck in my throat. I was terrified. I went to the washroom and splashed water, thrice, on my face. I have to wash thrice or else, I will not have peace of mind.

Suddenly, an idea, of how to get rid of the birds, flashed across my mind. I immediately filled my blue bucket with water and splashed it on the birds, who had been getting on my nerves, since the time I woke up. Hush! I felt relieved. I know, dear readers, that I had just vented out my anger on the poor birdies. I asked myself, is this the way a twelve-year-old girl is supposed to behave?

Then I flopped on my soft bed, started combing my curly brown hair, and laid down listening to my all-time favorite 'Shania Twain's song-'You're Still the One'. Listening to the song immediately calmed my nerves, as usual. While I was engrossed in listening, the door of my room swung open, like the mouth of the shark in the movie 'Jaws', which I had watched when I was just six years old. My beautiful mom entered, who is slim-figured unlike me. My daddy, on the other hand, is like me-chubby cheeks and dimple chin. I love to pull his cheeks. Even though my mom is in her early forties, she looks much younger than that. Credit goes to her non-stop daily morning yoga, which she never misses. She is fair-skinned, whereas, I fall into the wheatish category. I have always envied her enthusiasm; she is full of life. She knows how to enjoy every moment and always believes in living in the present.

Hey readers, don't panic. I am not going to bore you writing the whole book describing my mom.

"Hey, Bessie. A very good morning." She took off my earplugs and shook me hard.

"Still in bed?"

"Mom," I whined. "Those birds…!" Before I could complete my sentence, she, as usual, completed it for me.

"I know what you're going to say, honey. "Chirp-chirp of the birds! Am I right?" asked my mom.

"Cherish every moment, appreciate the little things. Don't waste time complaining."

Oh my goodness! I gasped, sweat trickling by. The same shrill voice again.

"Mom!" I called out.

"Did you hear that weird sound? Please do say yes."

"Nope," replied Mom, nodding her head and looking around my room.

"There is nothing, darling."

I couldn't tolerate my calm mother any longer, so I called out for my jovial, restless, and impatient dad. At times, these types of dads can be a supportive system, you know.

"Dad, Dad!" I screeched, at the top of my voice.

"Bessie, what happened?" Poor dad, he was at my door gasping and panting. He is the world's best dad.

"I have been hearing a strange voice since morning," I stammered.

"It seems like a bird, trying to tell me something."

"Come on, honey, relax. There are lots of birds outside our house, so it must be one of them," said Mom, quite worried and trying to cheer me up.

"Dear, stop reading too many fantasy and mystery books," joined my dad, sitting close to me.

"These are just creations of your imaginative mind and nothing else."

"I am not imagining, Dad," I insisted.

"Why do you refuse to believe me? I really heard a squeaky voice." I tried to imitate the squeaky sound like the one that I heard, but it turned out to be froggy. My bad luck.

"Am I going mad? Do you think so?" I looked at my parents with pleading eyes.

"Hey! Just relax. Nothing like that. You are fine, honey," said Mom, giving me a warm hug. Sometimes hugs do real wonders in your life, especially when they are from your parents.

"Thank you, mom," I said, tears pelting down. My dad, on the other hand, went to the corner, where I keep my dolls, and picked up my favorite baby doll, which I call Saisa. He knew that Saisa always made me happy. Parents are parents after all.

Dear readers, always love and respect your parents, no matter what; this much I know. I am always grateful to God for having such loving parents. Just when I was having very nice thoughts regarding my parents, Mom dumbfounded me with the news of the day.

"Get ready, dear. Your cousins are coming over for lunch."

"But why?" I burst out. I know it was a very stupid question, but I just couldn't help myself from asking.

"What type of a question is that, honey?" asked my mom, a little surprised.

"I invited them over for lunch. It's been a long time since we had a family get-together."

Whew! I huffed, under my breath. How can I forget that Mom is a social butterfly?

"Mom, you know, I hate parties," I grumbled, wrapping myself with Winnie the Pooh quilt.

"Cousins are boring. I hate mingling with them."

"Honey, it will do you good," piped Dad, giving me a gentle pat on my head, as if I was a little shy puppy.

"Dad, what good will it do? Tell me," I asked, looking into his eyes.

Even he knew I hated get-togethers. "You guys know very well I love staying in my cozy room all by myself."

"We know very well, sweetheart," said Mom, holding my hands.

"It is not healthy to stay cooped up in the room. We want you to mix up with people. Talk to your sisters. Tell them what is in your heart, like girly secrets. Hope you're getting me."

"Mom, do you know what you are saying?" I asked her, my face startled.

"Do you think I am an idiot to share my secrets or whatever you call it, with someone who even doesn't understand me."

"Jane, let her relax. Let her think for a while," said my dad to mom. Jane is my mom. I clasped Saisa tightly and just couldn't stop tears from rolling down. It fell on Saisa's cheeks also; it seemed as if she was crying, too, along with me.

"Please, leave me alone," I said under my breath. Saisa understands me better comparatively. I knew that I had hurt my parents, but I was feeling very helpless at the moment.

"Bessie," said Mom, holding my hand. "Will you just do a teeny-weeny favor for your mom? I won't force you, though." I nodded, hugging Saisa tightly.

"Will you at least join us for lunch? Your cousins would love to meet you." Silently, they left the room, leaving me with a big question mark. Whether to go down for lunch or not? Good gracious! I wished life wasn't so complicated. I wished I had a magic wand that once I spun, I would get all the answers.

"Magic is inside you, Bessie; you just have to find it on your own. Answers are all within you. Life is very simple, but we make it very complicated."

The same eerie voice resonated around my room. This time it called out my name. Good heavens! I covered myself from head to toe with my quilt, holding Saisa tightly. I went off to sleep again.

2:00 P.M. LUNCHTIME

Thud! Thud! Smash! Bang! Bang! Got you! Yahoo! Can you guess? What is happening, guys? You hit the nail on the head. These are the sounds and noises the little monsters are making downstairs. The party was in full swing. I was still in dilemma, whether to join the group or not. I am terrible at taking decisions. With the noise the little devils were making, I could neither concentrate on my new book, 'Goosebumps', sleep, listen to music, or draw. I was just sitting on my bed, motionless like a statue.

"How about joining your cousins, and having a bit of fun, instead of getting bored here."

The same chirpy voice rang in my ear again.

"Hey!" I shouted, looking up at my starry ceiling.

"Instead of scaring me to death, why don't you show yourself?"

"Definitely dear," answered the voice, "but on one condition."

I took some time to reply to whoever it was. Accepting the challenge was better than staying clueless. I had no choice.

"Done," I replied.

Whoosh! The pink curtains of my room started swishing. I got extremely scared. I clung tightly to Saisa.

"Gosh! What is happening?" I said silently under my breath. I was perspiring, like a pig. "Please show yourself immediately," I pleaded, almost in tears. "Don't frighten me." To my happiness, a pleasant smell of marigolds embraced me, in fact, my whole room. Suddenly a brightly colored, itsy-bitsy, adorable bird swooped in front of me, flapping its wings. ZAP!

Oops! I whooped and fell from my bed, Saisa on top of me.

"Who are you?" I stuttered, puzzled.

"What are you doing in my room?"

"Bessie, you asked me to show myself, so here I am," said the Birdie. Oh yes, that's what I am going to call her, Birdie. My secret friend Birdie.

"So, it was you all the time?" I asked, getting up and not getting scared this time, thinking it was just a little harmless Birdie.

"Yes," chirped Birdie, hopping on my head.

"Hey Birdie, you even talk!" I said, jumping in glee.

"I talk only with special children," replied Birdie, floating above me.

"What's so special about me?" I asked, picking up Saisa from the floor.

"As time goes by, you will find out," chirped Birdie.

"Your initial task is to join your cousins."

"Come on Birdie, it's not fair," I said, stamping my feet.

"You are like my parents, forcing me to do things, that I don't want to do."

"Hey Bessie," twittered Birdie, "now you are backing away from the word you have given me, remember?"

"Right, then this was your condition, huh?" I said, squatting on the floor. To my amazement, I started falling in love with this strange creature I had recently met. I didn't want to disappoint her. Didn't know the reason why.

When I kept silent for some time, Birdie spoke, "Face the fear, dear."

This sentence hit hard. Yes, she was right. I was petrified to face the crowd, and talk with them, I didn't know how to deal with them.

I wondered how Birdie knew me so well?

"Stop overthinking. Just be original, be yourself. Take a long deep breath and run down the steps. That's all you need to do. Easy-peasy."

After Birdie spoke, I looked at her small beady eyes and asked, 'Can I call you, Birdie?"

"Yes," chirped Birdie and flew away through the window.

2:00 PM, FAMILY GET-TOGETHER

I was doubtlessly a foodie. As I ran down the stairs, I was drawn towards the mouth-watering food, that was placed on the table. The dishes were extremely irresistible. There were my all-time favorite chicken and cheese salami sandwiches, popcorn, my mom's favorite egg salad, mushroom, and olive pizza (guys, to be honest, I detest olives), dad's favorite granola bars, veggie chips, chips chilies, yummy cheese cut in all shapes and sizes. Relax guys, I won't go further than this, except how could I forget to mention, that there were different flavored ice-creams as well.

Whew! I was exhausted. After scrutinizing all the delicious food items, I moved my eyeballs hither and thither. I was embraced with the same fear, what do you call it? Social anxiety. My cousins looked like giant dragons, baring their teeth, ready to devour me any moment. One lanky lady was rotating her fingers so much, that I felt a witch was standing in front of me, warning me to go back to my room. Sweat started trickling down. The word that I had given Birdie slipped from my mind. I decided to go back to my room when....

"Hey honey, I knew you would join us," called my mom, giving me a peck on my cheeks. I looked at her with a cheerful face, as I didn't want to ruin her party. I just nodded.

"Great," she said, holding my hand; God knows where I was being taken to. Kids were jostling, shoving and pushing each other. They were having a blast.

Smash! Boom! Thud! Crash! Doesn't this sound familiar to you guys? A crystal blue vase crashed into pieces. Oh! My God! My mom was just rooted in one place. She was flabbergasted. The vase was exceptionally precious to her because her husband had presented it on their anniversary. I was just waiting for my dad's expression. It would be worse than Mom's, I was dead sure.

"Baby, baby. What did you do?" cooed the little monster's mother, who had broken my parents' 'hearts' into pieces. Baby, I muttered. The girl looked like a Humpty Dumpty to me. The situation was pretty chaotic, but I couldn't help myself sniggering, remembering my favorite character-Humpty Dumpty. I loved drawing him when I was four.

Poor mom! She was trying her best to control the tense situation. She tried to pretend as if she was fine, whereas I knew she was bleeding from the inside. Mom was applying 3 C's formulae:

COOL, CALM AND COMPOSED.

I was fuming with Mom. Instead of scolding the girl for her monstrous behavior, she gave her a handful of chocolates instead. Life is unfair! I mumbled. My mom needs lecturing, I thought. A serious one. I was just seething with anger. I went towards my mom and pulled her aside, "Mom, instead of scolding the little brat, why were you pampering her? I know that vase is very precious to you."

"Honey, I know," said Mom, wiping her forehead with a tissue. "Sometimes remaining calm is the only choice one has sweetie. Relax."

"Mom!" I called out, "Mom!". She just walked away. The situation returned to normalcy. Invite more cousins, I grumbled under my breath. They are nothing but trouble. With my favorite drink, that is, a chilled watermelon juice, I went to a corner and flopped on my yellow beanbag. When I looked outside the window, I could see my Birdie perched on a branch. She looked very special, different from others. I should rather say, extra special.

"Birdie," I called out, waving my hand. "Come in. I need to talk to you." To my amazement, it didn't take even a second for her to appear in front of me. "OMG, I didn't see you coming," I chimed, feeling euphoric.

"Why are you sitting all by yourself?" chirped Birdie, "Go and chat with your cousins."

"Birdie, I don't like mingling with them," I insisted. "Don't know the reason but I have found a friend in you because you understand me. Can't we chat here instead?"

"We can chat anytime, Bessie," said Birdie, "but if you mix up with others, you will get out of the fear that has been haunting you all these years." Birdie was right. In reality, I didn't want her to leave me alone.

"Hello! What's up! Why are you sitting alone here?" intruded my fifteen-year-old talkative cousin, Stephanie. She really was a tattler. She was the last person I wanted to come across and here she was. I looked for Birdie, but she had already left.

"Can I sit here?" Stephanie asked, pointing towards a small wooden chair. I nodded my head, sipping juice. She knows very well that I don't get good vibes from her, but still, she loves bugging me.

"Tell me, what's going on in your life, Bess?"

"What about you?" I asked, loathing every single moment.

"It's wonderful, Bess," replied Stephanie, slurping orange juice.

"Guess who's my latest crush?" As if I wanted to know, I muttered under my breath.

"Who?" I asked hesitantly.

"Oh! It's Sam," she cooed.

"I can write a novel about him." So, guys, you can very well imagine my situation. Stephanie bored me to death, with her non-stop chattering about the 'so-called' Sam. I almost dozed off. Bless my mom, she called us for lunch.

"I will tell you the rest of my story later, Bess," said she and stormed off. Without saying anything I joined the others for lunch. I was starving, having lent my ears to the non-stop babble regarding Sam. If he appears in front of me, it will not take me half a second to strangle him, even though he hasn't done any harm to me. After lunch was over, I kept annoying my mom, asking her if I could go to my room. She looked at me and smiled. "Thanks, Bessie. You can go."

I ran up the stairs, as if zombies were chasing me and slammed the door shut. Goodness! I missed you my beloved room. I am genuinely lost without you. I plonked myself on the bed. What a relief!

"Thanks for joining the lunch dear," twittered Birdie.

"Hey! Birdie, don't scare me like this. At least give me a warning before coming. I guess, I should tie a bell around your neck," I giggled. "Then I will know of your arrival."

"Next time, I will surely warn you before coming," said Birdie, hovering in my room. I didn't believe it though. Just looking at its colorful wings gives me peace and happiness.

"I had a tough time, with my cousin Stephanie," I groaned.

"Thank heaven, mom turned up in time."

"At least, you got an opportunity to listen to the opinions of different people," said Birdie.

"If you stay alone, you'll not be able to know people."

"C'mon, Birdie, why is it imperative for me to know people when I am happy on my own?"

"Tell me, Bessie, why do you go to school? Why don't you do homeschooling?"

"I wish I could," I said, hugging my pink teddy, Maggie.

"I enjoy the company of Pinky, so I go to school. I want to meet her every day."

"See," said Birdie, finally perched on my bookshelf.

"People are social animals. They need friends."

"Your talks are making me bored, Birdie," I said yawning.

"You seem like my Maths teacher. I don't understand what he teaches,"

"Don't you ask for an explanation when you don't understand?" chirped Birdie. I nodded, twirling Saisa's wavy hair.

"Why?" asked Birdie. She was not going to leave me until and unless I answered.

"Because once I had asked, and the whole class laughed at me," I replied, remembering the incident.

"That was your mistake," said Birdie.

"Superb, Birdie! I thought you were my bestie and here you are, blaming me," I said, a bit hurt.

"I am not blaming you, Bessie," replied Birdie, skipping on my blue 'Disney Princess' carpet.

"What I meant was that you should have asked again, ignoring the class dear. These small incidents should not bother you. It will never help you to move forward in life. Don't give your remote control to others. You stopped asking, and your friends bullied you more. Maths became your least favorite subject. Show people you are not petrified of this world, let people be, what they be, if they be."

Good gracious! Birdie took a deep breath.

"You are correct, Birdie. You are my lifesaver," I said.

"I think this much is sufficient for today," said Birdie.

"Have a wonderful time and ponder over what I have said, dear. Last but not least, before I leave. You must make an effort to become happy." Whoosh! Birdie flew away.

9:00 PM

I was reading a book. Trying! Trying! My phone buzzed. I leaped at once, closing the book. I knew who it could be at that moment.

"Pinky!" I screamed as soon as I picked up the phone, startling the poor girl,

"Is everything okay?" asked Pinky, sounding a bit nervous.

"Have a chill pill," I said, grinning.

"It just seemed like ages since I had spoken with you."

"You gave me goosebumps, Bessie," said Pinky.

"How was the party?"

"I somehow dragged myself. Thank God it's over," I said, yawning.

"Get ready for another one," said Pinky. I didn't say anything for a while. Eventually, I found my voice.

"What do you mean, Pinky?"

"I am organizing a small slumber party in my room," said Pinky.

"Don't tell me I have to join you!" I said before she could complete her sentence.

"Obviously, Bessie! The party will be incomplete without you," said Pinky. "You are my bestie."

"Are you my best friend or my enemy?" I cried out.

"You know very well I don't like parties."

"Come on, Bessie, it will be just a few girls, please don't say no," Pinky pleaded.

"Can't you do without me," I pleaded too, like a mouse does with a cat.

"Come on don't be a wet blanket", said Pinky, losing her patience.

"You can't spend the rest of your life in your room."

"It's my life and I will do as I please. Stop giving me lectures," I slammed the phone. Clasping my Teddy, I couldn't control my tears. I grumbled, why don't people leave me alone?

"I think you need to talk with me," twittered Birdie, appearing suddenly as usual. I was happy that at least I had Birdie, who understood me.

"I think I hurt Pinky," I said, with tears still pelting down.

"True friends always understand, don't worry," consoled Birdie, hovering around. I kept quiet, just nodding my head.

"Pinky knows I hate parties, still she is insisting me to join her," I groaned. "That's what true friends are for," said Birdie.

"Don't talk in riddles," I said, getting aggravated.

"You know very well that I am not in the right frame of mind at present."

"Pinky wants the best out of you," chirped Birdie.

"She wants you to be a carefree girl, unafraid of crowds, and to be able to face obstacles which may come in your way."

"Do you think so?" I asked Birdie, wiping my tears, with a tissue, that was on the bed.

"I am positive," answered Birdie.

"Now pick up the phone and tell her that you'll be joining her teeny-weeny slumber party." I took a deep breath,

"Will she forgive me?"

"Trust yourself," said Birdie, signaling me to pick up the phone. Without further delay, I picked up the phone and blurted out, "Pinky, yes I am coming."

"Great!" Pinky was Pinky after all. She was squealing and laughing, and hopping around, whatnot.

"Fabulous, darlings," screeched Pinky.

"See, it was so easy," said Birdie, flapping its wings in a lively way.

"Why are you still sad Bessie?"

"Birdie, I still don't think you understand me," I said, twirling Saisa's curly hair.

"I have never been to any 'Slumber Party' before, Crowds always make me sick. I had to agree because I don't want to hurt either Pinky's or your feelings. I am sure the party will bore me to death."

"Bessie," Birdie perched on my beanbag. "Thank you for respecting our feelings. Until and unless you go, how can you assume it will be boring? Who knows, it might be exciting too. Just try it, dear. My advice is go, enjoy, experience, and then decide whether you want to return or stay."

"So easy for you, huh!" I said. "Easier said than done, Birdie."

"Trust me this time," said Birdie and soared away. I pondered for a while. Maybe Birdie was right, I must go to this time. If I don't like it, I can always come back home. With these thoughts, in my mind, I switched off the lights and decided to go to sleep.

6:00 P.M. SLUMBER PARTY

"Birdie! Birdie! I need you very badly," I called out, opening my window. I needed to talk to her, before going to Pinky's house for the 'Slumber Party'.

"Birdie!" I screamed my lungs out.

"Have patience dear," chirped Birdie, as usual appearing out of nowhere. Now I was getting used to it; she could appear out of nowhere.

"I have no clothes for the slumber party" I grumbled. "What to do?"

"When will you say you have sufficient clothes?" teased Birdie, fluttering its wings.

"Never," I said, grinning from ear to ear. That was the cardinal truth. Even though I bought clothes frequently, I felt I never had enough. I think this is every girl's feeling, am I right?

"Open your cupboard. I will help you to choose," said Birdie, perched on top of my cupboard. "You are my sweetheart," I said, blowing her a kiss. When I opened my Barbie cupboard, heaps of clothes toppled on the floor.

"If this is the way you keep your clothes, how are you going to find them," said Birdie, now perched amid my clothes.

"Come on, stop adding fuel to the fire," said I, plonking myself on the bed.

"Don't worry. I will arrange this mess later. First, help me decide what to wear."

"Bessie, if you keep your things organized, your life too will become organized, remember this," said Birdie, still glued amongst my mess (clothes). I had no choice except to nod my head. Finally, we decided, that I'd go for the 'Minnie Mouse' night suit, which my mom had bought for me during her last visit to Bangalore. I had forgotten about this night suit. The best part about the night suit was it had a black, long tail too.

"Remember what I have said," chirped Birdie.

"I will," I said and decided to get ready with thousands of thoughts reeling in my head.

8:00 PM, PINKY'S HOUSE

The massive iron gate at Pinky's house was opened by two bulky guards. My heart was playing hopping and catching as I repeated a mantra, which Birdie had taught me 'You are going there to enjoy, not to impress people.'

"Yes!" I said to myself, pretty loudly. My dad looked at me and asked, "Babydoll, are you okay?"

"Yes," I stammered going scarlet suddenly. The car stopped and it seemed for a moment that my entire world had stopped too. Slow as a turtle, dragging my Teddy, Maggie, I came out of the car. At that moment I wanted to tell my dad, don't leave me here, just take me back home, but I decided to give myself a chance.

"Have fun darling," waved my dad, and drove away. Gathering my guts, I headed towards Pinky's big bungalow. For the first time, I counted the steps while climbing up the stairs. My legs turned into jelly, as I reached her room. My whole body froze. My head started spinning. I could hear chuckles, titters, and laughter coming from Pinky's room. This discouraged me even more from entering the room.

"What are you thinking, Bessie? Just take a deep breath and go in," chirped Birdie. I looked around wondering where the sound was coming from, but she was nowhere to be seen. I took a deep breath and entered the room. I saw three girls hitting each other with pillows. The music was very loud. Snacks were placed on the table. I looked around for Pinky, but I couldn't trace her. Sweat started dribbling and I became breathless. I told myself, no, I cannot do this. I came out of the room silently. I asked myself, how am I supposed to spend a whole night with these girls whom I don't know? What am I going to talk about? I was tempted to call my dad and snuggle in my cozy bed with Maggie.

"Where are you, Birdie?" I called out.

"I am in a dilemma. Please help me."

"I am right inside you," called out Birdie, from somewhere within me.

"Be confident and face them, Bessie. You can do it. Remember, this moment will not come again. Just grab it."

I didn't say anything for some time, just listened to whatever Birdie was saying. Eventually, I decided to face the girls.

"What are you doing at the door?" asked Pinky.

"Come in."

"Yup," I said and slowly followed her. I always loved Pinky's room. Her favorite color being blue, she had everything in blue, from curtains to walls. I glanced at her bed sheets, they, too, were sky blue. Her walls were full of her favorite singers. I was pleased to see our picture at the center of the wall, framed in a golden color.

"Girls, girls. Stop pillow fighting," Pinky yelled.

"She is Bessie, my best friend." I was standing in front of them as if I was a renowned Hollywood Star.

"Hi Bessie. I am Ananya," a tall girl in polka-dotted shorts with Winnie the Pooh tee came forward to shake my sweaty hand. She was extremely beautiful; wish I was as beautiful as Ananya, I mused. "Be happy as you are," chirped Birdie. "Thanks Birdie," I mumbled, "Please be with me throughout the party."

"Hey! You seem lost," said Pinky, waving her hands in front of me. "Um…nothing," I stuttered. Panda, on the other, was somewhat like me, short, chubby, and fair. The difference was that she was far more confident. She knew, what she wanted in life. She had a habit of twirling her hair all the time.

"Nice to meet you, Bessie," squealed Panda, hugging me. Oh god! I could never be friendly with strangers at first sight. She was bold, I thought.

"I am Nancy," a pixie-looking girl introduced herself. I found her like the character from Enid Blyton's books. She seemed shy and demure. I couldn't help liking her frozen princess hooded night suit.

"Guys," said Pinky. "Now make yourselves comfortable while I fetch creamy hot chocolate for you." "Shall I come too?" I asked in a pleading tone.

"Be comfortable, dear. I will get it," said Pinky, winking at me. I wanted to run from the situation, but I knew. She was leaving me with the strangers purposely. All of us flopped on the Harry Potter carpet and for a while, didn't know how to start a conversation. I just kept munching Lay's chips that were on the plate.

"Are you fine?" Ananya asked me.

"Fine, no worries," I replied. I didn't want them to see my true self. I was wondering why Pinky was taking ages, to get hot chocolate.

"Hot chocolate, guys!" screamed Pinky. Think of the devil and there she was. This time, she was like God to me, not a devil. I felt a bit relaxed after she came.

"Now, what plans do you have, guys?" asked Panda, sipping hot chocolate.

"Hey, let us enjoy hot chocolate first," said Ananya. "We have the whole night."

"It's yummy," said Nancy, sprawling on the floor.

"Why are you so quiet, Bessie?" asked Panda.

"Oh, it will take her some time," said Pinky squeezing my hand. I looked at her and smiled. I mumbled, "Thanks."

"Let's play games, shall we?" said Nancy. "I have an idea," said Pinky, pulling her jumbo teddy and hugging it.

"What?" all of us asked together. I started feeling a bit relaxed. I thought maybe Birdie was right after all.

"What about 'truth and dare'?" This was the worst game for me. I was giving daggers to Pinky, but she pretended not to notice it.

"Wow! Excellent idea!" said Panda, almost spilling juice all over me.

"Don't we need a bottle for that?" asked Ananya, clasping her hands in glee.

"Oh yes," said Pinky, "Don't worry girls." She got up and fetched a Coke bottle to start the game. All of us sat in a circle.

"Birdie," I whispered. "Are you there?" I didn't hear any answer. Stupid, I groaned. My heart started hammering again. "Just a game, Bessie, relax. Go with the flow," said a voice from within. "Birdie!" I screamed, elated. Everyone looked at me, wondering what had happened; I went red like a beetroot.

"Uh…nothing," I said, with a smile.

"Shall we start the game?" asked Pinky.

"Oh yes, I am extremely excited," said Panda, gobbling popcorn as if she had not seen popcorn for decades. The bottle spun and spun, and at the same time, my head was going round and round. Good golly, Miss Molly, to my dismay the bottle stopped right in front of me. My ill-luck! My whole body became cold like ice. "Bessie, Bessie!" everyone yelled, clapping their hands.

"Are you fine?" said Pinky, looking at my face.

"You look as if you have seen a ghost." Ghost was better, I mumbled.

"Okay, girlie," said Panda, "Truth or dare?" Why was she in such a hurry? I got irritated. Should I pick Dare? I mused. A big 'No', I muttered, with bated breath. It would be too risky. "Truth," I blurted out, trusting the universe.

"Wait, wait, guys. I will ask her," said Pinky, with full enthusiasm. I was astonished. To see my bestie taking the initiative. For the first time, I tried to be positive. Maybe she was saving me from the others. She will give me the easiest question, like what's your favorite color.

"Who is your crush in our school?" asked Pinky. I was dumbstruck when she bombarded me with this question. I felt like I had been stabbed in my back. I had not expected this at all from Pinky.

Hoo! Teased the girls. My eyes were brimming with tears. I couldn't utter a single word. I just wanted to shut myself in my room, with a good book. I was detesting every moment. I hated Birdie for encouraging me to attend this horrible party.

"Bessie," I could hear a soft Birdie voice within me.

"Go away," I groaned, "You put me into this situation."

"Dear Bessie, life is a game, play it well. Don't show tears to these people. Tears are your weakness. This is your chance to show you can outwit them." Suddenly, I thought, Birdie was right. I would not be a crybaby. I will outsmart them. I wiped my tears with the tip of my fingers and faced the girls with a different outlook.

"Casper!" I answered, my head held high. Inside, I knew I was a bit nervous, but I was trying not to show. Pinky was amazed ath my pretty bold answer. I refused to look at her. I was still fuming with her for putting me into that situation purposefully.

"Wow! Really?" chorused the girls.

Casper was two years senior to me. He was every girl's dream boy. I went to school early just to get a glimpse of him. Once when he said, 'Hi' to me, the whole night I couldn't sleep.

He was tall, cute and had dimples; how could I miss those green sparkling eyes? "You did it, Bessie," said Pinky, squeezing my hand.

Maybe she was feeling bad about it. But I just nodded, still hurt with her. The bottle spun again. Everyone waited with anticipation. Ananya! The girls whooped. This time I screamed, too.

Thanks to Pinky, she had unlocked the key to my heart. I was now enjoying the game, finally. "Dare!" said Ananya, without waiting for us to ask her. Maybe she was mentally prepared. "Me, Me, I will ask her," said Panda. I was enjoying the show. Socializing was fun, no doubt, but not always, "Shoot!" said Ananya, Crossing her legs. Panda tumbled down the stairs and fetched two eggs. I was already reading Panda's mind. I just hoped I was wrong; Was she going to break those eggs on her head? Or was she supposed to eat them raw?

Yucks! "Take these eggs and crack them on your head," sniggered Panda. See, I knew it. My mouth went wide open. Didn't know how many bacteria would get a chance to enter my mouth. As far as I knew, Ananya was fond of her long lustrous hair. Will she do it? I thought. Pinky was far better I guessed. Bless her. Instead of truth or dare, this should have been named as the 'Revenge Game'. Nancy covered her mouth, trying not to laugh. "Are you mad?" asked Ananya "I have just washed my hair." "Dare is Dare," said Pinky, grinning.

I could understand how Ananya was feeling, and had just one word for it- disgusting! Reluctantly, Ananya took the eggs, trickling up her face and without Delay, cracked the eggs. I covered my eyes.

I couldn't see the state she was in. The yolk was dripping down her face and her silky hair had become sticky. "Oh! My gosh! My hair!" she screamed. "It's gummy." "Sorry Ananya, it was just a game," said Panda, giggling. Ananya got up immediately to wash her hair and face. To be honest, I was not enjoying the game, like the others were. Anyway, the bottle once again started spinning after Ananya returned. Lo and behold! It stopped in front of Pinky. How could I forget to avenge myself, Guys? "Go for dare, if you dare," I challenged her. I knew her weakness. She hated challenges. She accepted quickly. "Very well. Done," said Pinky, with a shrug. I, too, ran down the stairs, excited like a little girl for her first Christmas gift, fetched ice cubes. From the fridge. "I can very well guess what you're going to make her do," said Nancy, rubbing her nails "Oh! Yes. You're right, chuckling, "Put these inside your tee."

"Are you nuts?" Pinky asked, shocked. "Dare is dare," bellowed the girls. I knew Pinky was not happy with me. Serves her right, for being mean to me, I said, under my breath. Pinky held the ice-cubes In her hands, closed her eyes. And put it inside her 'Disney Princess' tee-Shirt. Pinky stopped dead. Her lips started trembling. I held her hand; it was freezing. I felt a bit guilty, for making her choose 'dare'. "Hey. Are you okay?"

I asked, a bit worried. "I am fine, guys," said Pinky, coolly." scooping out ice cubes from her tee. I knew she was trying to be cool, whereas underneath, she was ice cold. Well, anyway, all's well that ends well. "I never saw this side of you," Pinky whispered to me.

"I am sorry," I said, with a smirk "Come on, all's fair in a war and gamea," said Pinky, giving a pat on my back. Now only two players were left. Nancy looked nervous, I noticed; she was perpetually nibbling her nails. "Me?" she whispered. "Truth or Dare?" asked Ananya. "Truth," said Nancy quickly "Have you ever lied to your parents?" asked Panda. The question was so quick that I didn't even have time to blink.

"Um...," Nancy stuttered. "Yes once." "Only once?" teased Panda rubbing her hands. "Spare the poor girl," said Pinky, "she has gone scarlet out of fear."

"At least, tell us what did you lie about?" prodded Ananya.

"Do I have to answer?" asked Nancy, looking at us.

"Obviously," said Panda, taking a huge bite of the pizza. It took a whole ten minutes for Nancy to answer. All of us had gone really restless. Pinky had asked the others to spare her, but Panda and Ananya remained stubborn. In fact, even I was curious to know what she had lied about. Nancy seemed really gullible to me, in person. Eventually, she spoke. Thank goodness. "I had jumped out of the window, kissed my crush and climbed up the ladder back to my room and slept." "What?", croaked Panda, she dropped the half-eaten pizza on the floor. I looked at Pinky, her mouth was agape.

"Did you really do that?" asked Ananya, pinching herself. "I cannot believe it. You never told us." "Yes," said Nancy, her eyes brimming with tears. "This is the only thing that I have hidden from my parents." The game wasn't a game anymore. It had turned emotional. Nancy started sobbing heavily. Maybe she had been bottling up in her heart, all these days. "He', it's all right," said Panda. "You did nothing wrong. Forget it. Chill." "Let me give you a hug," said Pinky and gave her a big hug. Didn't know why, but when Pinky hugged her, I felt a twinge of jealousy.

Panda was the only one left. "What should I go for?" asked Panda, looking around us.

"Can you see that attractive guy sitting on the fence?" asked Ananya. Panda looked outside the window. "Yes, but I 'haven't said truth dare, as yet." "Honey, you have no choice," grimaced Ananya. "Definitely 'Dare'". I chuckled; I knew Ananya was taking a revenge on her. Truth or Dare was surely becoming a fun, no doubt. "So?" asked Panda, "Do I have to go and kiss him?" All of us covered our mouths and giggled. Panda had a heart of a lion. "Will you be able to do it?" challenged Ananya. Without speaking a word, Panda left the room. All of us looked outside the window. We could see Panda speaking with the boy. The boy seemed to be fourteen-years old. He had brown curly hair, and was wearing brown shorts and a white tee. I wondered what was he doing at that hour. "Hey," I asked. "Did I miss something, Pinky?" I had been so engrossed in my thoughts that I'didn't come to know whether Panda kissed or not. "I did it!" cried out Panda, barging inside the room like an earthquake. "Cool, huh!!" said Ananya, with her hands on her hips. "You kissed him on his cheeks."

"Hey! What do you think? I am going to kiss a stranger sprawling on his lips," said Panda, on the floor. "I will save that for Mr. Right."

Hoo!! We hollered. Birdie was somewhat right, I thought. 'Slumber party' was, in fact, becoming fun. "Shall we watch a nice movie?" suggested Nancy, curling up with a comic that was lying on the table. "Not a bad idea, but before that let's enjoy the food," said Pinky.

"I am starved," Pinky was right. I was hungry as well.

Pinky's mom was very fond of cooking. You just have to name it and she would make it. Wow! It rhymed. The glass top table was filled with potato chillies, chicken pizza, tuna sandwiches, slices of cheese, cucumber vegetable patties, hot dogs and, last but not the least, white forest cake.

'Let's dive in," I said, unable to resist the lip-smacking food. I let the girls yap and yap as I enjoyed eating and listening to their sweet and sour non-stop chatter.

"Wow, I feel really good after eating," said Panda, getting up and stretching herself.

"Now, guys. how about a movie?" asked Nancy.

"Cool," said Pinky, bringing her laptop.

"Shall we watch 'Klause'? I had been wanting to watch this with you girls." I had already watched this movie on Netflix, but I didn't mind watching it again. A very inspiring movie. The girls agreed. We cuddled up in the bed, laptop in the center. I was feeling very strange and uncomfortable. I had cuddled up with my parents or my plushies, but never with friends.

"Are you all comfortable?" asked Pinky, looking at me.

"Oh yes" I said, hugging my Maggie. Panda kept a bucket of popcorn in front of her. Amongst all of us, she was the foodie, I was hundred percent sure. The movie 'Klause' was on. I was relating myself to the characters of the movie. 'Klause' was sent to an unknown place, where he didn't want to go, like I had come to Pinky's house, even though I didn't want to. The girls were giggling, shoving each other, pelting each other with popcorn. I was lost in my own world of imagination. I was happy being me. Finally, the movie ended.

"It was one of the nicest movie, I have ever watched," said Nancy, giving us her big yawn.

"C'mon," said Ananya. "Stop being a drama queen."

Snowy was Pinky's pup. It was Japanese Spitz. Pinky loved keeping Snowy with her on her bed. Snowy became everyone's toy. She, too, was loving the attention she was getting.

"Stop, Snowy, you are making my face sticky," said Panda, wiping her face. All of us couldn't help tittering at the amusing sight. Eventually, Snowy quietly sat on my lap.

"I am sleepy already," yawned Nancy.

"Hey, wake up," nudged Pinky. "I have something planned for you all."

"This is fun," said Ananya, playing with Snowy's ear.

"Come on, say it fast,"

"We have to find the things, listed in this slip," said Pinky, spreading the list on her bed.

"Even I am clueless about it, because my mom is behind this game." "We trust you." Said Panda, patting her almost toppling Pinky from the bed.

"Whoever finds it first will be the winner," said Pinky.

"What fun!" clapped Nancy.

"I love these kinds of games." I also kind of liked the game because there was minimum communication to do.

"Girls are you all ready for scavenger hunt?" asked Pinky, giving each one of us small slips.

"Uh-huh!" we shouted. I looked at my list carefully, checking the things I had to find.

1. Spiky
2. Book
3. Sticky
4. Coin
5. Heart
6. Red
7. Rubber band
8. Rubber

While my head was still glued to the list, the rest had already started hunting for the treasure.

"Bessie, did you find something rough?" asked Nancy. "Anything spiky?" I asked. Both of us looked at each other and laughed. Didn't know the reason why suddenly I saw something dangling in Pinky's small flowerpot "Oh yes!" I said to myself. "Rubber band." I crossed out rubber band from my list; it was a big victory for me.

I looked at the others. It was surely a funny sight; Nancy was trying to go underneath the bed, Panda could be seen dancing in happiness, Ananya was trying to get hold of a slimy kind of a thing, but it kept on slipping by, Pinky was inside her wardrobe. Guys, you must be wondering what I was doing. I was also trying to find the items as soon as possible. To my luck, I saw a green stuff, lurking from behind the curtain.

"Whoopie!" It was a cactus. The spiky item was crossed out from the list. I asked myself, had Pinky's mom really meant cactus? Oh my goodness, how am I going to hold it? The voice within said, "Bessie, you can do it." Suppose I pricked my fingers? I was really in a dilemma when I felt a thump on my head. It was Panda, "What's up?" she asked. She understood me without saying a word.

"Hey, Bessie, that cactus is just a toy. It won't prick you."

"Are you a mind reader?" I asked, a bit relieved. Come on, anyone can say looking at your startled face," giggled Panda.

"You were having a heart-to-heart conversation with that fellow." I felt embarrassed. Silently, I picked up that so-called fellow and kept it in the plastic bag given. I looked at my watch, time was elapsing by really quickly. Just a few seconds were left for me to find the things that were in the list. I looked around at my friends, Ananya's plastic bag was already full. It seemed she had found all the stuff. Nancy was still lurking around.

"Did you find everything?" Pinky poked me from behind.

"What about you?" I asked, looking at the plastic bag which she was carrying. "Just these two things." She showed me a small butterfly clip and a smiley fridge magnet.

"Time is up," Pinky's mom called out from the door. Pinky's mom was a very cheerful lady. She was involved in some kind of a social organization. Her motto in life was very simple- eat and be happy.

Ananya was declared the winner. Pinky's mom placed a cute pink crown on her head. I was sure the crown was made by her mom, because as far as I know, Pinky is not creative at all. Ananya also got a whole big packet of snickers as a gift.

"Don't tell me you're going to eat it all alone," said Panda, trying to snatch the packet.

"I'll give it to everyone, except you," said Ananya, grinning. Each of us got two snickers. I ate one and saved one for home. After all, the scavenger hunt was enjoyable. I was not ready for another game; I was eager to hug my teddy and go to sleep. I looked around; it seemed the girls were still in high spirits. I couldn't help myself giving a big yawn. Thud! Ouch! Guys! Can you guess what happened? A pillow fell right on my face. It was Pinky, obviously. I, too, picked up the pillow and hit her hard. Within no time, our pillow fight started. I forgot all about my sleep. It was really entertaining. Panda smacked Ananya so hard, she fell on the floor from the bed. Ananya grabbed another pillow and hit Panda on her face. I took a pink cushion and smacked Pinky on her butt, and she landed on top of Nancy. "Gosh! You squashed me," whined Nancy. Pinky wouldn't spare me, I knew. She asked all the girls to hit with several pillows, while she held me tight.

Whew! It was really fun. No wonder, it's said that a slumber party is incomplete without a pillow fight. Eventually, all of us, lay flat on the bed, laughing to our heart's content. I had never laughed so much like this in my life.

"Hey, Panda, will you get me a glass of juice?" asked Ananya. To my surprise, without answering back, Panda fetched juice for her.

"Thanks dear," said Ananya, with a grimace.

"I am not getting up anymore, huh," said Panda. "I am very tired."

"Anyone interested in dancing?" asked Nancy.

"Are you nuts?" asked Ananya.

"I am dead tired."

"Fine. Nancy will dance. We will watch," I said. I didn't know how my voice opened out.

"If you join me, I will dance," said Nancy, playing with her hanky.

"Yup. We'll join you later," said Panda, winking at me. I felt good to be included in the group.

"Promise," asked Nancy. Pinky pushed her from the bed to the floor and put on a dancing number. We couldn't help laughing, seeing Nancy dancing. Her steps were so funny, and her face was extremely hilarious. We couldn't stop ourselves from encouraging her to dance more. "Once more, once more." We clapped. After Nancy stopped, Panda joined her, and she entertained us with her another whimsical step. I knew she was purposely trying to make us laugh.

"Oh, Panda. You are such a darling," cooed Ananya. Pinky pulled me to dance with her. I didn't hesitate. I had started feeling very comfortable with the environment. I didn't try to entertain anyone. I just danced to make myself happy.

Birdie had said, "Be original." For the first time in my life, I enjoyed it very much. Thanks to Nancy and her funny steps. I looked at my watch; it was already 1:30 A.M. OMG! I had never stayed up so late in my life.

"Guys, guys," said Pinky, waving slips in front of us. "I have a last game before we retire to bed, shall we?" We were too drained out to disagree with her idea. I have written things on each slip. Each of you has to pick up a slip and do what is written."

"What about you, sweetheart?" asked Panda.

"I knew this question would arise," grinned Pinky.

"You guys decide for me,"

"Done," said Ananya, picking up the slip.

"Wow! Someone is interested, huh!" teased Panda.

"Walk like a model," was on the list. I thought that was easy-peasy for her. Hoo! We howled like foxes. My parents should have seen this wild fox side of me. They would have been super-duper thrilled and impressed. Ananya got down from the bed and immediately walked exactly like a model.

"Wow! I knew it," I screamed.

"You were just amazing," I gave her a big pat on her shoulder.

"Thank you," said Ananya, sheepishly.

"Come, Bessie, your turn," said Pinky.

"Fine," I said, confidently. Reading the lines made my eyeballs pop out. My confidence vanished into thin air.

"Call your crush and say 'I love you'."

"No, it's not fair."

"I can't do it." I whimpered, lips trembling.

"Come on, it's only a game," said Panda.

"You were the one who chose the slip, after all." I looked at Pinky, with pleading eyes, hoping she would rescue me, but she was in high spirits that day. My feet started becoming numb. I was frozen. I became dumb, speechless; the girls were looking like vampires to me, with their fangs all set to suck my blood. My heart started thumping, and hammering, and sweat trickled by. I became totally deaf.

"Hey, what are you contemplating, about?" Pinky asked, waving her hand, in front of me.

"I can't do this," I mumbled under my breath. But no one heard my plea.

"Be fearless," said Panda, clapping and slowly everyone joined her.

"I know who is in your mind," said Pinky, nudging me I gave her a 'Why are you doing this to me?' glare. She was too euphoric to understand my feelings. Suddenly deep within, I could hear Birdie, chirping,

"Bessie, it's just a game, play with a smile. Don't be a victim, be a victor." Thank you, Birdie, I mumbled. I took a long and deep breath and said, "I am ready,"

"That's my girl," said Pinky. There were butterflies in my stomach. I was feeling nervous, too. I still remember those green eyes, picking up my books, which I dropped in the library. Those eyes still haunted me. Tring! Tring! Oh! My goodness! The phone started ringing. I clasped my cell phone tightly. I didn't want the girls to hear my throbbing heartbeat.

"Helloo!" a husky voice answered.

"Helloo!" I yelped in a jitter, dropping the phone. The girls were tittering. Shush! Pinky asked them to be quiet.

"Who's this?" the voice asked. My hands were trembling. My mouth refused to co-ordinate. I thought I had lost my voice.

"Bessie," I whispered. Before my crush could say anything, I just blurted out, "Casper, I just called to say, I love you." Please forgive me, I was mumbling under my breath. Thud! I hung up the phone. I was gasping for air. I was wiping my sweaty head profusely.

"Hey! You did it," everyone clapped. I looked around me, they were laughing and enjoying themselves, but I wasn't feeling comfortable. I felt like puking. My head started to ache.

"Drink this, you'll feel better," said Pinky fetching lemonade for me.

"Come on Bessie, just chill. It's just a game."

"Pinky, I need to go home," I uttered suddenly, tears rolling down. I felt guilty too, for spoiling her party but it was too much to handle for me.

"Bessie, we are sorry," apologized Panda, holding my hand.

"Please, don't go," pleaded Pinky, almost in tears.

"I am extremely sorry," I didn't know what happened. I started sobbing loudly.

"Pinky, just drop me home," I whimpered like a small girl. Pinky called her driver and without saying anything to anyone, I rushed to the car. I knew I was going to regret this later because I had jeopardized her party completely. But what to do that was the real Bessie after all.

8:30 A.M. MY ROOM

"Bessie! Wake up! Sweetie!" My mom was waking me up.

"Oh, Mom let me sleep for a while," I grumbled.

"Come on, remember, we have to go to our Aunt Lee's place for lunch."

"Oh, mom, you guys go. I am not in the mood to go."

"Bessie, this is the third time you'll be denying her invitation," my mom was trying to convince me. Aunt Lee was a chubby lady in her forties. She and my mom had been friends for decades. She asks my mom to bring me along every time she invites us, and I always come up with excuses. This time, I promised that I would go on one condition, that she buy me a Barbie with a pink dress, which I had been eyeing for a long time.

Poor her! She had no choice except to agree. After I sent Mom from the room, I clasped my teddy and started crying, thinking about the previous night's incident. Pinky must be mad at me, for ruining her party. I was ashamed to face her. Windowpanes rattled fiercely, and lo and behold, just when I needed her, Birdie swooped inside the room, flapping its colorful rainbow wings. She settled herself on my bookshelf, facing me.

"Oh, Birdie! I missed you," I cried, clasping Maggie tightly.

"I am a coward. Everyone is right, I am not made for this world."

"Bessie, it's all right," chirped Birdie.

"You are a human being. It's fine to make mistakes, but do not repeat the same mistake. Learn from it." Whatever Birdie was trying to explain, nothing went inside my thick head.

"Birdie, what are you trying to tell me?" I asked, getting up and crossing my legs.

"Instead of complaining about what went wrong, why don't you think it over, and focus on what went right?" said Birdie, hovering around the room. I couldn't think of anything that went right in the party. I was just feeling guilty for ruining Pinky's well-planned party,

"Fine, let me ask you something," said Birdie, perching back to my bookshelf.

"Did you enjoy the slumber, party?"

"Oh yes," I answered immediately, with a twinkle in my eyes.

"Why did you enjoy it?"

"Don't have any idea, Birdie," I shrugged.

"Please answer for me."

"Come on, you are the one who went, experienced, so how can I answer on your behalf?" said Birdie, hopping on my bed from my bookshelf.

"Fine," I said, with a slight smile on my face.

"To tell you the truth, I had never expected I would have had so much fun until that incident happened."

"Forget about that incident, cherish the beautiful memories only, which you made at the party," said Birdie, spreading its wings.

"You are right, Birdie," I said, wiping my tears.

"Do you know we played games, we had pillow fights, ate scrumptious food, and much more." I completely forgot about the painful experience while I was sharing my experiences with Birdie. I was totally in bliss.

"Birdie, I just wish I would have stayed longer, instead of returning home,"

"Just relax, Bessie," said Birdie.

"This is called life. Don't think too much. Just think that at that moment, whatever you thought was right, you did it. Don't ever blame yourself. Pinky is your bestie. She will understand."
"But Birdie, suppose she doesn't?"

"Forget supposing, be positive, and enjoy the present moment. Enjoy the little things that you have in life."

"Birdie you always know how to bring a smile on my face," I said, clasping Maggie after Birdie flew away. I pondered over the conversation we just had; I felt much better.

5:00 PM IN MY ROOM

Whew! I am exhausted, I sighed flopping on my plush bed, flinging my blue Minnie haversack on the beanbag,

Tring! Tring! My phone buzzed. I was about to go to the washroom to freshen up. Tring! It rang again. I looked at my cell phone. It was an unknown number. My parents had strictly warned me against picking up unknown numbers. I was ambivalent about whether to pick it up or not. I decided not to. It rang again and again, continuously. I thought it must be someone I knew. I decided to pick it up,

"Hello," I said. There was silence at the other end.

"Hellooo!" I said a bit louder. This time, someone did speak. Guess what, guys? It was a boy's voice.

"Hi Bessie." Good heavens. I was very much familiar with that voice. It can't be, I thought. I pinched myself several times to be assured that I wasn't dreaming. I dropped my phone in nervousness and picked it up again.

"Are you there? Is everything alright?" the voice asked.

"Yes yes, I am very much here," I stuttered. I stood like a statue, with the phone against my ear. Numb, dumb, anything you name it, that's what I was in that situation.

"Is that you, Casper?" I asked, finally finding my voice.

"Yes, of course," said Casper, "Why? what happened?" That killer voice, I grimaced. Wait till the girls hear about it. They will go crazy.

"How did you get my number?" I asked.

"Hey, remember you were the one who called me?" grinned Casper.

"Oh yes," what an idiot I was. I had forgotten about the slumber party incident. He had saved my number. Both of us remained dumb for a while, not knowing what to say.

"Won't you say anything?" asked Casper. I was so mesmerized by his voice that I didn't know what to say.

"Casper, I am sorry about it. We were playing games and…" Before I could complete my sentence, he said,

"Yes yes, I can guess the rest of the story. You fell into the game trap, right?"

"I am sorry," I apologized again.

"But it was a beautiful trap," Casper said.

"I kind of liked it."

"Didn't you mind?" I asked stunned.

"Why would I mind such silly things?" said Casper. Wow. He is super cool, I thought. I had been feeling guilty for no reason.

"I thought I would surprise you by giving you a call," said Casper.

"Surprise? I was shocked," I said tittering. Both of us were silent again.

"Can I call you sometimes?" asked Casper. "If you don't mind." How could I say no to such a sweet lovely melodious voice?

"Yes," I squeaked, getting elated like a mouse getting a big chunk of cheese.

"So, bye for now," said Casper.

"Till then, stay safe." I wanted to hear his voice always.

"Bye," I said reluctantly. Pinky Pinky, I yelled at the top of my voice. You must hear this. I jumped on my bed. I dialed her number but unfortunately, she didn't pick up. I will tell her later, I told myself. With happy, happy thoughts reeling in my mind, I ran down the stairs for quick snacks.

9:30 PM

My schools were in front of me, but I was not able to concentrate. Casper's husky voice was still ringing in my ears.

"Birdie, oh Birdie. I wish you were here now. I want to share my feelings with you," I said, hugging my rag doll, Meesha.

"You remembered me and here I come," chirped Birdie. I looked around but couldn't find her.

"Birdie, where are you?" "Look under your bed," twittered Birdie. I jumped from my bed and looked under my bed; there she was gently perched on the carpet.

"What are you doing there?" I asked her, beaming.

"Do what makes you happy, and that's what I am doing," replied Birdie, flapping its wings.

"Your statements are very difficult to understand sometimes," I said sitting cross-legged.

"There is something interesting to tell you,"

"Do you like Casper?" asked Birdie, coming out from under the bed, and soaring above me.

"Oh my god! How can I forget that nothing is hidden from you," I said, as Birdie hopped around the room.

"Your face shows you are very happy," said Birdie. I stood in front of my oval-shaped pink mirror. I looked closely at my sheepish face. I noticed that I looked stunning; no wonder people say, that when they're in love, they look beautiful.

"Keep on smiling like this," said Birdie, perched on my bean bag.

"You look fabulous."

"Thank you, Birdie," I said with a bow. I felt at that moment I was over the moon.

"Do you think Casper likes you, too?" asked Birdie, perched on my bean bag. There was a pang of fear in my heart.

"He likes me, Birdie," I replied, plonking on my bed.

"Or else, why would he bother to call me? Please don't scare me Birdie." My face immediately changed into fear.

"Come on, no need to get upset. Go with the flow and control your emotions. As you are aware, you are very sensitive, and minor things disturb you. Just be careful. Prevention is better than cure," Birdie said. Birdie was right, I always used my heart rather than my head, and that's why I have suffered in life, "Birdie, if you permit me, should I call Casper?"

"No way," said Birdie firmly. I had never seen this firm part of her.

"Let him call, have patience, dear. Listen to what he has to say. Listen more, talk less."

"Okay okay, Birdie, enough for today," I said, getting irritated.

"Remember my advice. Don't tell me later that I hadn't warned you." With these words, Birdie flew away from the window. I laid down on the bed and started thinking, why did Casper call me? Does he like me too?

2:00 PM SATURDAY

"OMG! Bessie! I really cannot believe it!" screamed Pinky on the phone,

"You have a date with Casper. The hottest guy in our school. You will be every girl's envy." "Yes," I screamed back. You heard it right. I have a date with the hottest guy in the school. I am just waiting for the girls' reaction.

"Yes yes," Pinky screamed. "Lucky girl."

"Hey, speak softly, my ears are splitting," I said, covering my ears.

"Did you tell your parents?" Pinky asked.

"Oh, they will be over the moon," I grinned. "You are the first one."

"What did he say, when he called you for the date?" asked Pinky.

"Come on, I want to know everything."

"Um," I stammered. "Nothing as such. He just asked whether I was free or not, and I replied yes; that's it."

"Next time don't say yes to everything," said Pinky.

"Hey, are you jealous?" I asked, looking at my recently painted pink nail polish.

"Come on, spare me. Why should I be?" said Pinky.

"Just teaching you a few tips, don't be available all the time. Guys will start taking advantage of you."

"Cool. Relax," I said, avoiding argument. After hanging up the phone, I decided to take a beauty nap for some time and dozed off.

4.00P.M.

Tap! Tap! I rubbed my eyes. I was in a deep sleep. Who would be tapping on my window, I thought. I got down from the bed, dragged Maggie, and pulled the curtain.

To my utter joy, it was my precious Birdie, flapping its wings. Birdie has something to tell me. "Hello-Birdie," I said, as I opened the window.

"Someone looks happy today," twittered Birdie, perched on my bed. "I know why."

"Tell me why?" I asked, trying to get hold of her. She flew away. She never lets me hold her. "Why don't you let me hold you? You are so beautiful."

"Beautiful things are to be admired, not to be touched," said Birdie, perched on top of my closet. "You and your riddles," I said, clasping my doll Saisa.

"Tell me, Birdie, which dress should I wear for my date? I am very confused," I asked, opening my wardrobe and scrutinizing my heap of clothes. "Simplicity is your best attire," said Birdie. "What do you mean, Birdie?" I asked, "Please don't confuse me with riddles. I cannot go as a hermit." "Fine. Close your eyes and pick," said Birdie.

"No way. I am not going to take a risk. If I end up choosing undies," I imagined myself in my undies. and couldn't help myself from chuckling. "You and your funny imagination," said Birdie, hovering around the room. "What I am talking about makes sense," I insisted. "You are giving me weird ideas." Birdie flew near my cupboard and pecked one of my favorite blue frocks. "Wear this," said Birdie,' "It's your favorite." "I know, Birdie, but it's too simple. Should I borrow a cute dress from Pinky?" I asked,

"I know she has hot ones, perfect for dates." Birdie remained silent for a while. I knew I was going to get a lecture.

"Bessie, try to be content with the things that you have. If you keep becoming dissatisfied you will end up unhappy,"

"I knew you would say this," I said, flopping on my bed.

"Never try to look beautiful by wearing other's clothes,"

"But Pinky is my bestie," I insisted, "What's the harm in borrowing?"

"Just imagine, Bessie, if unintentionally you happen to tear the dress on your date. What would happen? Have you ever given a thought about it?" Birdie asked me. I kept quiet. I didn't say anything.

"Birdie, I would never be able to face her.

"Instead of enjoying the date, the whole time you'll be worrying about the dress,"

"Oh yes," I said remembering an incident when I had lost her favorite earring. She had become mad at me.

"You are right, Birdie," I squeaked, "Then you decide for me what I should wear."

"Tell me, what do you feel comfortable in?" asked Birdie, perched on the carpet.

"Jeans and tee," I said immediately.

"Then go for it," chirped Birdie.

"Are you nuts?" I asked shocked. "Going on a first date in jeans, that also with the hottest guy?"

"Bessie, let me tell you, don't pretend what you are not. Be original, like I always say; your inner beauty matters, not the outer,"

"This doesn't mean Birdie that I should go in rags?" I complained.

"Go in jeans and wear some trendy tops," suggested Birdie, fluttering its wings.

"You will look incredible, trust me. People will judge you on how you think and how you behave and not on what you wear."

"Hey, Birdie, at least do you agree that I must look presentable?"

"Of course, I don't deny that," answered Birdie. Before I could badger Birdie with more questions, it flew away. I clasped Saisa and mused over what Birdie had told me just now. I stood in front of my closet and took out my black faded jeans and pink Disney princess tee. I am done, I told myself. Life is simple, we make it complicated. Birdie's sweet voice echoed in my ears.

1:20 PM SUNDAY, LUNCH WITH CASPER

"Are you nervous, honey?" asked my dad driving the car.

"Dad, I am not in the mood to answer," I said, looking outside the window of the car,

"Come on, relax, you'll be fine on your date," said Dad, beaming.

"Your mom was also nervous on her first date."

"Was mom nervous?" I asked Dad, looking at him with enthusiasm. I have always thought mom to be a very strong woman, and I was surprised when I came to know that she could be nervous, too.

"Then how did she handle it?" I asked Dad. I thought a small tip might help me.

"Just go with the flow," said Dad. Concentrating on his driving. I tried to remember where I heard this phrase earlier.

"Oh yes, Birdie!" I cried out.

"Birdie?" questioned my dad, looking at me confused.

"Um, nothing Dad. I guess we are getting late," I tried to change the subject.

"Come on, honey," said dad.

"You will be prompt for your date," finally we reached our small dating spot.

THE NEST

Do you like the name guys?

I jumped off the car, like a small girl eager to meet Santa Clause. As soon as Dad stopped the car, he shouted, "Have fun, sweet pea."

"I will," I yelled back. I consoled my dad that I would enjoy the date. Little did he know how nervous I was. As I was clambering up the stairs, my hands started sweating. I couldn't find my heartbeat. I was trying to remember the lessons Birdie had taught me.

Whew! My head was just revolving. I just didn't know what my reaction would be when I saw his face.

Casper was seated in the corner. Oh Goodness! He really was a handsome boy. He had come in light blue jeans and a white T-shirt, where it was printed, 'DARE YOU TOUCH ME'

"Bessie," he was frantically waving his hands to me. My legs were jammed to the floor. They refused to budge at all. I was strung high. Dragging my body, I reached him eventually. My first words were "Sorry, I am late." Oops, I did it again. Maybe I will die in his arms saying sorry.

"It's all right, relax," said Casper, grinning, pulling a chair for me.

"You are looking beautiful."

"Really?" I yelped, forgetting for a moment that I was nervous. I was dying to hear these three magic words from his mouth. Wish I could have recorded it. Maybe next time.

"What are you smiling about?" asked Casper, drinking water.

"Um, nothing," I replied, blushing. So far, so good. I breathed.

"What do you want to eat, Bessie?" asked Casper, looking at the simple menu card.

"Anything," I replied, trying my best to be polite. This was not me. When I am in a restaurant, I am a picky eater. If I were with my parents, I would have gone for pizzas, prawns, the list goes on. I remembered that I was on a date. I had googled it that guys don't like girls who eat a lot.

"Shall we order chicken pizza?" asked Casper.

"Wow!" I whooped, "I love pizza."

"I can see someone's eyes twinkle," teased Casper.

"What about drinks?"

"Let's go for a smoothie," I suggested this time.

"Great!" Casper said, closing the menu.

"Bessie, why don't you tell me something about yourself."

"What do you want to know?" I asked a bit anxiously.

"I mean, what do you do in your leisure hour, blah, blah.." Casper replied, sipping his mango smoothie, which the waiter had just served. The service was very prompt in 'The Nest'.

"It's yummy," I said slurping the smoothie.

"Don't try to change the topic," Casper smiled. I wondered what I should tell him, should I tell him that I talk to Birdie, a friend I made recently, or that play with dolls, watch cartoons, and movies, or sleep or daydream when I am bored? No way! He would surely run away from me.

"I love reading," I said, taking a bite of the pizza,

"What are you reading at present?" Has he come for a date, or come to take my interview? While thoughts were reeling in my head, I choked. Casper got up and patted me on my back.

"Drink water," said Casper, giving me half –a glass of water.

"Thanks," I replied, gulping down water.

"Don't worry, I am fine," Thank God, I choked. Both of us remained silent for some time. Finally, I found my voice, "Casper, why don't you tell me about yourself?"

Before answering, Casper cleared his throat and said, "I am Casper and I love flirting,"

"Are you serious?" I asked, looking at his face, wondering whether he was joking or was he serious.

"I am positive," replied Casper grinning, showing his well-set teeth. The color of my face started changing from white to pink to blue to red.

"You seem to be angry," said Casper, laughing,

"I was only joking,"

"Come on, I don't like these kinds of jokes," I said almost in tears.

"I am sorry, henceforth no more pulling each other's legs, okay?" said Casper, making a pathetic face. I just couldn't help laughing looking at his face. It was hilarious. After that, both of us laughed, spilling the rest of the mango smoothie on the table.

"Woah! Bessie, I enjoyed our first date," said Casper, holding my hand.

"Me too," I replied, shyly.

"Will you be my girlfriend?" Gosh, it was like my dream come true. I will be the center of attraction in the school, every girl's eye will be on us. We would be awarded the best couple at the school.

"Hey! Where have you got lost?" asked Casper, nudging me. "You haven't answered my question."

I nodded my head slowly with a sheepish smile.

8:00 PM DINNER TIME

"Bessie, eat your food slowly. What's the hurry about?" Mom scolded me, serving the spinach. My most detestable vegetable.

"Honey, tell us how your date went?" asked Dad, chewing the juicy chicken.

"It was fabulous, but I will tell you in detail later," I said, gulping down water and trying to swallow the rest of the food that was on my plate.

"Bessie, I can very well understand why you are rushing things," said Mom, serving herself a spoonful of salad.

"You can go to your room."

"Oh, thanks Mom," I said, blowing her a kiss. I ran up the stairs and slammed my room door shut. Slam! Whew! I sighed, taking out my cell phone. I looked at the phone umpteenth time. Casper had said he would call me sharp at 8:00 p.m. What if he doesn't? I asked myself. Was he just pretending to like me? How will I face the situation, then? I was having numerous weird thoughts, and just then…tring..tring…, my phone started buzzing. I whopped-

"Hi, Bessie." Wow! Casper, I am just in love with your voice. I mumbled, clasping my phone, tightly.

"Bessie, are you there?"

"Oops, sorry," I apologized.

"I was waiting for your call,"

"Did you have supper?" asked Casper

"Yes, just finished," I replied, playing with my hair.

"Are you done with your schoolwork?"

"Oh, I will do it after talking with you," answered Casper. "Guess what? I have already finished mine so that I could have plenty of time to talk with you," I said, looking at my Disney princess poster. There was a knock at my door.

"Just a second, Casper." It was my mom. She had brought a glass full of creamy milk, kissed me goodnight, and left.

"So, tell me, Casper, what's new?" There was silence at the other end.

"Casper, are you there?" I asked. There was no response. I was confused. I asked myself, had I told him to hang up the phone? I very well remembered I had not. Then what happened? I wanted to call him and ask, but my fingers refused to budge. I decided that I would ask him later. I changed into my orange panda shorts and snow-white tee, then got inside the bed. I took out a Harry Potter book and started reading, enjoying the creamy buttered milk.

3:00 PM

"Birdie, tell me something. Have you ever kissed anyone?" I asked, twirling Saisa's hair. Birdie was perched on my bookshelf.

"Yes," she replied, flapping its wings.

"Really?" I asked, mesmerized.

I never knew birds could kiss.

"Obviously. I have kissed my parents," answered Birdie, hopping down the shelf.

"You are so boring," I said.

"I meant to say a guy, you idiot,"

"Why are you so interested, Bessie?"

"Casper has been bugging me fordays to give him a kiss on his lips," I said. "As if it's a child's play."

It had already been a month since we had been dating and still hadn't kissed. Recently, Casper got annoyed regarding this matter and I don't want to lose him. Birdie didn't chirp for a while. She remained motionless.

"Have you become a statue or what?" I asked, pelting her with small cotton balls.

"Are you angry with me?" I asked, scared of losing Birdie.

"Why don't you say something? You are my best friend, that's why I shared it with you," I continued, eyes brimming with tears.

"Bessie," finally Birdie spoke.

"This is not your age to think of kisses and other stuff. Think of your goals and ambitions. What you want to become when you grow up. Think of outsmarting your friends, who thought you were good for nothing, and make your parents proud of you," Before Birdie could lecture me more, I intruded, "Birdie, kissing is also a part of life. If I don't listen to him, I might lose him. I have promised Casper that I will kiss him today during our walk. Please don't make things complicated for me,"

"Bessie, being your best friend, I want the best for you. Don't be ruled by your emotions. If Casper loves you, he will never leave you, remember my words. Don't crave physical attractions. Maybe you are too young to understand me now, but later on, you will realize how right your friend Birdie was," "OMG! Birdie, you overthink," I said, placing my hands on my waist.

"Nothing like that; Casper loves me. You just chill. Don't worry about me. Remember promise is a promise, Birdie."

Birdie perched on my snow-white quilt said, "If Casper loves you, he will respect your feelings. He will never force you to do things which you are not comfortable with." With these last words, Birdie gilded away, leaving me in a confused state. For the first time, Birdie was wrong I felt.

5:30 P.M. A WALK WITH CASPER

Casper and I had decided that we would meet in 'Whispering Park'. It was the best park for couples. I had once been there, with my parents. The problem, as usual, was what should I wear? I opened my closet and surfed through heaps of clothes. Eventually, I picked one of my favorite blue floral frocks. I decided to wear white sandals with it, which my mom had purchased for me. Perfect, I told myself, giving myself a slight pat.

"Casper is here, Bessie," my mom yelled from downstairs.

"Coming Mom," I yelled back. Hearing his name gave me butterflies in my stomach. I was wondering, how would I be able to kiss him. I stood in front of the mirror and looked at myself for the umpteenth time. Pinky had already given me a small lesson on how to kiss a guy. Hope Casper will find me a 'good kisser'. With thoughts in my mind, I ran down the stairs. As soon as I saw him, I hugged him, as if I was seeing him after ages.

"What's wrong? Hey, relax," he said, acting a bit strange. I thought, maybe because my mom was around, so he felt awkward.

"Have a blast," said Mom, patting me. She was my mom, after all. She knew that I felt hurt. The park was twenty minutes drive from home. Both of us remained quiet while the driver was driving. I was still feeling hurt by his weird reaction. Finally, he broke the ice.

"Bessie, did I do something wrong?"

"Nothing," I said, refusing to look at him, eyes full of tears. We reached the park. As usual, the park was full of people, especially couples. Some were seated under the bush, chit-chatting, some were opening gifts, and some were just strolling. Guys, you must be wondering what were we doing. We chose a corner, where there was a wooden bench. I was tempted to have cotton candy, which was my all-time favorite, but I didn't want to embarrass myself in front of him. The most beautiful part of the park was the fountain. I don't know but just looking at it gave me peace.

"Hey, Bessie, are you lost somewhere?" asked Casper.

"Oh! I was just looking at that fountain," I said. "I love it."

"Would you like to take pictures there?" asked Casper.

"Oh, great," I said, getting up. We went near the fountain. He took several pictures of me in different poses. I felt really good after that. I forgot that I was hurt by him just a while ago.

"Do you want ice-cream?" he asked me, pointing towards a stall selling different flavored ice-cream. Who would say no to ice-creams? I asked for my favorite black current. He fetched two ice-creams. While I was having the ice-cream, I could feel his hand holding mine. I got goosebumps. I thought how would I kiss him? Should I tell him that I am too scared? Will he understand me? The thought of losing him scared me.

"So, dear, what about the promise you had made?" asked Casper, after he had finished with his chocolate cup ice-cream. I knew he would remember it. I remained silent. My lips started trembling. I kept on twirling my hair.

"Don't you trust me?" asked Casper.

"Hey, please don't say that," I said, looking at his eyes.

"I trust you more than myself."

"Then why are you hesitating?" asked Casper, bringing his face a bit closer to mine.

"Just wait, Casper," I said. I pulled myself back. I took a deep breath.

"What's wrong with you?" asked Casper, a bit irritated.

"I have chosen a place, where no one can see us," I looked at his face. He looked so gullible and naïve. How could I deny his little demand?

"Just a small kiss, right Casper," I asked, hands shaking.

"Yes, a small kiss that's it," said Casper, smiling.

"Fine, I'll make things easy for you. I'll close my eyes," Those enchanting eyes made me go insane. I just had to kiss him. No matter what, I told myself. Without any delay, I just gave him a huge smooch on his lips. I did it! I did it!

I laughed out.

"You did it! You did it!" Casper yelled.

"You won Bessie! You are amazing!"

"Guys, guys! Stop hiding, show yourselves. See I had challenged you, I would win this bet," said Casper, standing on the bench. I felt as if I was being punched in my stomach. I saw girls and boys Casper's age, coming out of nowhere. They surrounded us and started clapping loudly.

"Casper, you did it," said a pixie-looking girl, kissing him on his cheeks.

Casper was looking at them and grinning ear to ear. He seemed shocked. It seemed it was part of a game.

"What's happening Casper?" I asked, not knowing, whether to cry or to be happy. It was like a nightmare for me. A tall and lanky guy spoke,

"Hey kiddo, do you really think Casper fell in love with you?"

"What do you mean?" I asked tears pelting down, continuously.

"Casper, why don't you say they are lying."

The same pixie girl spoke, "Casper had challenged us, that he will make you kiss him within a month."

"No, it's not true," I wailed, flopping on the grass. I jerked Casper so hard that he screamed.

"Stop it, Bessie. Enough. Didn't you hear them? They are telling the truth. Who would fall in love with a nutcase like you? Do you think I am a fool? By the way, honey, you are after all not a bad kisser," saying this, they marched out of the gate, leaving me stranded all alone. Birdie, I should have listened to you. You were absolutely right.

"Come home, Bessie. I am waiting for you," I heard a whisper from my Birdie.

8:00 PM, HOME

By the time I was home, it was 8:00 pm. I had called Pinky to pick me up from the park. I couldn't face my dad with my tearful eyes. When I saw Pinky, I hugged her and cried my heart out. I told her everything that had happened. She was seething with anger. Her face had gone red. "I am not going to leave him," fumed Pinky, wiping my tears. I didn't want any more drama in my life. I knew Pinky could be rebellious when she wanted to. I pleaded with her not to create any scene. After much coaxing, she agreed. Pinky's driver dropped me home. I was wondering what I would tell my parents. I took my steps towards home, very gingerly. My parents were in the living room. I looked at them, how happy they looked. I didn't want to spoil their happiness.

"Hey, Bessie. Why are you standing at the door?" asked Mom, "Come here," I couldn't control my emotions. I ran towards my mom, hugged her, and started sobbing.

"Hey, baby girl, is everything all right?" I couldn't say anything except shedding tears continuously.

"Honey, come and sit with Daddy," said Dad, holding my hand and asking me to sit beside him.

"What happened, dear?" asked Mom, sitting close to me. I told them everything that had happened at the park. Baby, this is called experience, said Mom.

"You have a long way to go," I expected her to get fumed with Casper, but she was as cool as a cucumber.

"Mom is right," joined dad.

"Don't waste these precious tears for worthless people. You'll meet many more good guys, don't worry, now smile."

"Shall we celebrate your 'Break-off' with ice-creams?" said Mom getting up to fetch ice cream. "Yes," said I, wiping my tears and helping Mom to bring ice cream.

IN MY ROOM

As soon as I entered my room, I plonked myself on the bed, Of course, my parents had tried to make me feel better, but inside, I was still hurt. I asked myself, how could Casper do this to me? I had loved him from my heart. Birdie, I am sorry, you were right. I need you now. To my relief, I heard Birdie, chirping.

"Bessie, I had warned you, hadn't I?"

"Yes Birdie, you had warned me," I said. I looked here and there for her, but she was nowhere to be seen.

"Birdie, where are you? Are you angry?" Just then, Birdie appeared, perched on my pillow. OMG! When I saw Birdie, I was very happy. I couldn't stop tears from pelting down."

"I am sorry, Birdie. I didn't listen to you. I used my heart instead of my head."

"Bessie, remember this is just the beginning of our life. You will face many more things in life. You have to learn to control your thoughts, learn to differentiate between right and wrong," said Birdie, still calmly perched on my pillow.

"Birdie, you know very well, that I loved Casper, I still can't believe that all these days, he was playing with my emotions," I said eyes brimming with tears,

"Bessie, you are just a young girl to understand the true meaning of love," said Birdie, flapping its wings.

"As you grow older, life will teach you what true love is. You just had an infatuation with Casper, and nothing else."

"Birdie, why me? What wrong had I done to him? The only mistake on my part was that I had trusted him wholeheartedly," said I, clasping my doll Saisa.

"Trusting Casper blindly was your biggest mistake," said Birdie, perched on the bean bag.

"You let your emotions rule over your head."

"Can you be a little bit clearer?" I asked, feeling better.

"For instance, you hardly used to give time to your parents, in order to talk with him; nor did you used to eat your meals properly; you even started rushing over your schoolwork. What about your goals? Have you ever thought about it? You even started ignoring your bestie, Pinky. Your world revolved just around Casper," chirped Birdie. I didn't say anything, I just listened quietly while Birdie spoke. Everything was becoming crystal clear to me. I started hating myself for being self-centered.

"Bessie, you even started bunking dance classes," said Birdie.

"This used to be your favorite hobby, am I right?" I just nodded, with tears pelting down.

"You are correct, Birdie. What shall I do now?" I asked in a hushed voice.

"How will I be able to face my friends?"

"Come on, Bessie, life doesn't stop here," said Birdie.

"Your life has just begun. Casper was an eye-opener. You got a chance to learn a lesson, but don't repeat the same mistake. You should actually thank him. Be a new Bessie, have a new outlook and a new attitude towards life, be confident and brave; no more timidness, no more crying over small things. Are you getting me?"

"You are my best friend Birdie," I said. "You always know how to make me feel cheerful. Believe me, I will try not to disappoint you." "Don't say try," said Birdie, perched on my windowsill.

"Say I can, and I will. A bright future awaits you with open arms," with these inspiring words, she flew away. I stood in front of my mirror, brushed my hair, and gave a big wide smile.

WELCOME TO NEW BESSIE!!

7:30 AM SUNDAY

Tring! Tring! I was woken up from my sleep.

"Hey, sleepy head! Wake up. Remember, we have to head for shopping today?" squeaked Pinky.

"I remember, Pinky," I said sleepily, looking at my alarm clock.

"You idiot! It's only 7:30, why did you wake me up so early?" I had been spending very little time with Pinky, so to make up with her, we had decided to go shopping.

"Because Princess needs loads of time to doll herself up," said Pinky, excited. Shopping always makes her happy.

"Cool, chill. I am getting up. Don't eat my head," I said grinning, feeling happy, thinking of spending time together. After a long time, I did everything in a jiffy. The shower was done, Brekkie was over, and I didn't take time choosing clothes, just picked whatever I could get a hold of-black shorts with a pink tee.

"Enjoy girls," waved my mom when Pinky came to pick me up. Pinky was looking super-duper cute in her floral blue skirt with a white top. Pinky's driver dropped us off at our all-time favorite shopping center.

BUZZING BEE MARKET.

BUZZING BEE

Buzzing Bee was the perfect name for the market. There was hustle and bustle everywhere. People were jostling each other; some were strolling as if they were in a park, and kids were pestering their parents to buy them toys.

"Bessie, you are lost in thoughts again," nudged Pinky.

"Wake up."

"Let me take a breath," I said.

"Fine, let's move."

So, we started hopping from shop to shop.

"Pinky look, I spy with eyes, a cute 'tank top'," I screamed, showing her a white spotter top with a unicorn printed on it.

"Wow! It's so beautiful. I want to buy it," yelled Pinky. We headed towards the shop. There were heaps of dresses. We were really in a dilemma, about which ones to choose and which ones to leave, as we had a limited budget.

"Bessie, wish we could buy the whole shop, isn't it?" said Pinky, fumbling through the T-shirts.

"Oh yes, yes," I said, elated.

"Look at those skirts."

Let's look at the skirts," Pinky said, keeping aside the tank top, for a while.

"Pinky, I am still eyeing that unicorn tee," I said.

"I think you should go for it," said Pinky. Finally, after much thinking, I decided to buy the unicorn tee. Without parents, shopping wasn't fun at all, this much I knew, as we would not have to worry about money at all.

"Bessie, do choose nice T-shirts for me," said Pinky, spreading heaps of T-shirts on the table.

"Wow, I love this Winnie-the-Pooh one with the blue background," I said, showing her the t-shirt.

"Incredible. You are right, Bessie," squealed Pinky.

"This is super-duper cute." Pinky ended up buying 3 tank tops, while I was happy with my unicorn tee.

"I need to buy a denim jacket as well," said Pinky. "Let's go to that shop, Pinky. I've seen sweatshirts too, which I need to buy," I said, pulling her hand. For the first time, we didn't have grown-ups with us, as we were sensing a feeling of freedom. The only crux was the limited amount of money. I spotted a pink hooded sweatshirt with Barbie printed on it. What more did I need? It was a little beyond my budget, but I couldn't resist the temptation. Pinky, on the other hand, bought a Denim Jacket and two pairs of jeans.

"Bessie, I am in love with those joggers too," said Pinky showing mr, in many beautiful colors. I needed a pair of joggers too, but it was quite expensive, so I decided to buy white cute shorts with blue butterflies printed on them instead.

"Pinky, I am really tired and hungry."

"Bessie, just give me a few minutes," she said, eyeing a few skirts which were on display.

"Come on, you have similar ones," I said. "Don't be an impulsive buyer."

"Do I have these skirts?" asked Pinky. She had so many dresses that she couldn't remember what she possessed and what she didn't.

"Look at this skirt, Bessie. I am dead sure I don't have this," said Pinky, showing me a pretty caramel one-piece dress with hearts printed on it.

"Oh yes, Pinky this is extremely beautiful," I shrieked.

"You must buy this without thinking twice." She purchased the dress.

"Bessie, do you like this heart-shaped necklace?" asked Pinky.

"No way," I said,

"It's too simple."

"Rather, take that heart-locked earring, let me buy it for you," said Pinky, trying it on my ear.

"Really?" I asked, excited. Pinky bought teeny-weeny earrings for me. I pulled Pinky to a shop where squish marshmallows were sold. I thought of buying her a gift. She was fond of plushies, especially squish marshmallows. Pinky got very excited when she saw different types of squish marshmallows of all shapes and sizes.

"Are you serious? You are going to buy one for me?" I asked Pinky, her eyes sparkling.

"Better choose the one you like, before I change my mind," I said, with a smirk. I had already guessed that she would choose the doggy one, with its flappy ears.

"Oh, thank you, thank you," Pinky hugged me.

"Most welcome," I hugged her back. After the shopping, we headed to our favorite café, 'Just Chill'. The waitress, who was in her early twenties, knew us very well. "Girls, chocolate chip ice cream?" Both of us nodded our heads, beaming. Within no time, our choco chip ice cream was laid in front of us.

"Enjoy girls," said Mary; that was her name.

"Yummy," said Pinky scooping out ice cream.

"What a wonderful time I had with you today," I said, holding her hands.

"Sorry for not giving you any time when Casper was not around," said I.

"Oh Bessie, forget about him," said Pinky, enjoying the ice cream. "What are besties for? By the way, have you checked out the new guy in school?"

"Oh, no. No more guy talks," I said. "Let's talk about something else."

"Come on, move on," said Pinky, "This world will be boring without hot guys. Casper was not meant for you. Be a sport."

"Cool," I said. "You are right."

"His name is Sugar," said Pinky, licking her finger, where there was a drop of ice cream.

"Sugar?" I asked. "What a weird name."

"That's his pet name; the girls have kept it for him," said Pinky.

"Our schoolgirls are crazy, you know. His real name is Roger," Pinky said, wiping her hands with a tissue paper.

"Wow, you've done enough research about him, huh," I teased Pinky.

"So what?" said Pinky with a shrug. "That's all I know about him. The rest you'll have to see for yourself when you meet him personally in the school."

I, too, got quite inquisitive to see the so-called Sugar.

"Hey Pinky, guess what?" I said, "My parents are buying me an iPhone."

"Wow! That's cool," said Pinky. "Congrats!"

"But there is a condition," I said. "I have to get A+ in all subjects."

"That's tough, huh," said Pinky, nodding her head. "I too had to slog a lot to get mine."

"These parents, they always have conditions with them," said Pinky, smirking.

"They never give us anything for free."

"What is your next demand?" I asked, scooping out the last bit of the ice cream.

"I am begging them to buy me the latest laptop. My pup has trampled on my old one ample of times."

"Wow, lucky girl," I said patting her.

"Just imagine, Bessie, no pocket money for these months," said Pinky, crinkling up her face, "Can you believe that?"

"You have me," I said, "I will lend you. But, in return, you'll have to lend me your laptop." Both of us had a hearty laugh. After paying the bill, we decided to head home.

"I detest going home after having so much fun," I said.

"Same pinch," said Pinky. "I have so much homework to do. Let's plan something for our coming weekend."

"Hey, I have got a brilliant idea," I said, twirling my hair.

"Movie?" asked Pinky. "Better than that," I said, my eyes glittering.

"Do tell fast. You know I hate surprises," said Pinky.

"What about camping in my backyard?" I suggested. "But just the two of us."

"Hey, great idea!" said Pinky, jumping. "We have never done that, smarty pants."

"So, done," I said, "Yup," said Pinky, giving me a high five. With the upcoming weekend plans in mind, we got inside the car.

5:00 PM

CONVERSATION WITH BIRDIE

"Maggie, I had a wonderful time with Pinky," I said, hugging my teddy. "Birdie, wish you were here now. I love to talk with you." I got up and opened the window, hoping she would come. I had forgotten that she could appear out of nowhere.

"Bessie, you remembered me, and here I am," said Birdie. I looked behind me, and there she was. Guys, I told you, she can appear from nowhere.

"You look euphoric, Birdie," I said, flopping on the bed.

"I am always happy," Birdie said, flapping its wings.

"Today I am especially happy because my Bessie is happy."

"Oh yes, Birdie, after a long time I am happy. I'd hopped and shopped until I had dropped."

"What did you buy?" asked Birdie, perching on top of my closet.

"Oh, wait, I'll show you," I said, getting off the bed. I still haven't kept it inside my closet. I showed everything I had bought.

"Do you like it, Birdie?"

"Of course, your choice is wonderful, Bessie," twittered Birdie, hovering around my things.

"Finally, you have started loving yourself."

"Now, Birdie, don't talk in riddles. You know it's difficult for me to understand," I said.

"What I mean to say is," said Birdie. "When you were head over heels in love with Casper, you had forgotten to take care of yourself. You had forgotten your true identity," said Birdie, perched on my unicorn tree.

"You are right, Birdie," I said. "Such an emotional fool I was. You opened my eyes, Birdie."

"You even started wearing clothes according to his taste," Birdie continued. I remained silent; how could someone be so blind and crazy in love? "Look at yourself, Bessie," said Birdie, still perched on my unicorn tree. "You look genuinely happy. You're glowing. You are finally doing things that you like and deserve."

"Oh yes, Birdie," I said. "You are correct. Thanks to you. I had forgotten myself. I love to eat ice cream, but I stopped eating for fear of getting fat. Mom used to scold me for not eating properly. I used to wait for his calls, instead of reading my books. How could I have been so foolish?"

"So, Bessie," said Birdie. "What I am trying to tell you is that there is time for everything. Try to balance everything. It is very essential to balance yourself."

"Oh Birdie, now you need not worry about me," I said, a bit tired of her perpetual preaching.

"What's your next plan, then?" asked Birdie.

"Guess what Birdie? We are planning on camping in my backyard," I said, clasping my hands. "Doesn't it sound exciting?"

"Wow! Great!" twittered Birdie. "I am extremely happy for you. Remain positive towards life like this. Always. If you laugh, the whole world laughs with you, but when you cry, you cry alone." Sometimes Birdie and her riddle become difficult for me to understand.

3:00 PM

A VISITOR

Today my mom invited Pinky and her cousin, Tiya, who had come to stay with her for tea. No wonder it's been a while, Pinky was not able to give me time like she used to. I wanted to meet her cousin, who was keeping my friend away. Suddenly out of nowhere, Birdie appeared.

"Hey, where did you pop in from?" I screeched.

"When my little Bessie was engrossed in thoughts," chirped Birdie, twittering its wings.

"Come on, Birde, sit in one place, don't irritate me," I said, flipping the pages of my book.

"Someone seems to be in a bad mood today," said Birdie, finally perching on my Barbie cushion.

"Birdie, tell me why should I be jealous of Tiya?" I blurted out.

"Who said you are jealous?" chirped Birdie.

"Your face clearly shows you don't like Pinky's cousin," Birdie chirped.

"Oh Birdie, sometimes I wish you couldn't read my mind so well."

"May I know the reason why?" asked Birdie, still perched in the same place.

"Come on Birdie, you know me so well, so why waste your energy asking me that," I asked.

"I want to know from the horse's mouth, too," said Birdie.

"Because Pinky spends more time with Tiya than me," I said with my head bent. But to my dismay, before Birdie could answer, Mom called out that Pinky and Tiya had come.

"I must go," I said to Birdie, but Birdie was nowhere to be seen.

"Bessie," my mom called out again, "Where are you?"

"I am coming," I shouted with a scowl.

I tumbled down the stairs as fast as my feet could carry. I was even very eager to meet Pinky's cousin, Tiya. Tiya was standing face-to-face with my mom and chatting away. She looked awesome and hot for a fourteen-year-old girl. She was in black shorts with a blue tank top and grey flip-flops. Her hair was sleek and straight. She was like a porcelain doll to me.

"Hey Bessie, meet my cousin, Tiya," Pinky introduced, holding my hand.

"Hey Bessie," said Tiya moving her hand forward to shake mine. I reluctantly moved my sweaty hand forward to shake her well-manicured one.

My, unlike me, was a very confident person. She always made the guests feel comfortable, she knew when, where, and what to talk about. When we were seated in the living room, I looked at them.

They were laughing and chatting at the same time, enjoying the delicious snacks. Whereas I, on the other hand, was lost in my world of imagination. I didn't know what to talk about. I was motionless and speechless, like a dumb statue. Then my superhero dad made his entry.

"Hey Bessie, why are you so quiet?" At that time, I felt like throwing a glass full of water to bring him to his senses. Everyone's attention quickly fell upon me, thanks to Dad.

"Bessie, uncle's right, you haven't spoken a word," said Pinky. "Is everything okay?"

"One needs an audience too," I said sarcastically.

"Yes, she is right," laughed Tiya. I know she was trying her best to make the environment friendly. Can you believe me guys, I did not speak a single word during the entire conversation. I was sure that Pinky was mad at me. Whew! Eventually, it was time for them to leave. I whooped under my breath.

"It was nice meeting you," I said to Tiya. Pinky gave me a 'really?' kind of glare. I smirked and returned to my room.

6:00 PM

Tring! Tring! My phone buzzed. I leaped because I was engrossed in reading an interesting book by David Williams called 'Blunders'.

"Hi, Pinky," I said, trying to sound cheerful, even though I was still feeling uncomfortable after meeting Tiya.

"What were you doing?" Pinky asked.

"I was reading," I answered.

"Great," said Pinky and kept silent. For the first time in our lives, we were feeling uncomfortable with each other.

"It seems like you have something to tell me," Pinky said. I knew I would be caught.

"Um, nothing," I hesitated.

"I know you very well, Bessie," said Pinky. "Stop lying to me."

"Seriously, there's nothing," I replied, eyes full of tears. I didn't want to hurt her by telling her the truth.

"Anyway, Bessie, how about lunch tomorrow? Just the three of us?"

"Three?" I asked, surprised.

"Obviously," said Pinky grinning, "Have you forgotten Tiya who is here with me?"

"Oh yes," I said taking a deep breath. She had completely slipped out of my mind.

"Pinky, if you don't mind, I don't want to join you guys for lunch."

"But why?" asked Pinky. "Give me a reason, why do I always have to force you to do things, Bessie?"

"Then don't force me, leave me alone," I said, tears pelting down.

"Tell me something, why are you acting so weird?" asked Pinky.

"Ask yourself this question," I said.

"Me?" said Pinky, "What have I done?"

"Since Tiya has come, you haven't given me time," I said, tears coursing down.

"OMG, Bessie! I never expected this kind of childish behavior from you," fumed Pinky, "Anyway just let me know if you are coming over for lunch or not."

"Let me think, and then I will let you know," I said and hung up the phone. I clasped Maggie and started sobbing. I looked at my phone several times, expecting it to ring, but it didn't. I had made Pinky angry, I thought. I was clueless about what had gone wrong with me.

"Birdie, Birdie," I called out, wailing. "Please help me. I need you. Please come. I think I have lost my bestie Pinky too!"

Birdie tell me more...

"Bessie, don't worry, you haven't lost her," said Birdie, appearing in front of me.

"Oh Birdie, I am so happy to see you. What will I do without you? Please don't leave me."

"Bessie, I am right in front of you," chirped Birdie, fluttering her rainbow-colored wings.

"Birdie, I hurt Pinky," I said, shedding tears.

"I am very sad. She had called me for lunch, but I refused her invitation,"

"Why don't you want to go?" asked Birdie.

"You know very well why, Birdie," I said, "I don't feel at ease with her cousin."

"Tell me something Bessie, has she done something to you? I mean to say, any harm?" I remained silent for a while, and then nodded 'no'.

"Then, what is the reason?" asked Birdie.

"Come on, you know everything, still you are badgering me with questions," I said feeling quite irritated.

"Yes, I know, Bessie," said Birdie, perched on her favorite spot, the Barbie cushion.

"It is very essential to know by yourself first. Who are you? What is it you need? What upsets you?"

I racked my brain for some time but could not make head or tail of what Birdie had said.

"Did you get me?" asked Birdie, "What is the particular thing that is upsetting you?" "Oh, this question is easy. I don't want Pinky to hang around her cousin," I replied immediately.

"This shows you have no problem with Tiya, right?" asked Birdie.

"Yes, I have no problem with Tiya," I said. "Pinky is giving her more time compared to me, that is what I am agitated about."

"This clearly shows you are being selfish Bessie," said Birdie, perched on my bookshelf.

"Birdie, this isn't fair, isn't it?" I said wiping away my tears.

"You are blaming me for nothing. How can I be selfish? I give her so many gifts. I share everything I own with her."

"Just giving away things doesn't make a person sensible and selfless Bessie, but in fact, understanding your bestie's situation is the best gift you can give to the person," said Birdie.

"But...Birdie, I always thought I understood her," I said, still confused. "Can you explain to me by giving an example?"

"Cool," said Birdie. "What I like about you is that you always try to mend your mistakes."

"Thanks," I blushed. I am very bad at taking compliments.

"When you were having a marvelous time with Casper," continued Birdie. "Just think it over carefully; did Pinky ever irritate you, complaining that you were not giving her time?" I tried to recollect those days; I used to forget to call Pinky, and deny meeting her during break times, but she always remained with me. Remembering those days made me weep loudly, "You are right Birdie, I am a very selfish friend. I always think of my happiness. Now Pinky is cross with me. I am sure she will never forgive me."

"Hey, hey, relax," said Birdie, hopping on my carpet.

"Pinky is not angry with you at all, trust me. She loves you very much. Just give her some time to think," said Birdie.

"Now what should I do, Birdie?" I asked, eyes full of tears.

"Easy," said Birdie. "Ask for forgiveness and go for lunch. Compromising is necessary in every relationship Bessie."

"Oh yes! I will surely do it," I said, wiping my tears. "Thank you, Birdie, for making me realise my mistake."

8:00 PM DINNER

(AFTER LUNCH WITH TIYA)

"How was your lunch with Tiya?" asked Mom, pouring herself a chilled glass of water. She was aware that I was not at ease in her company the other day.

"Dad, Mom," I said slowly. They looked at me, wondering what I was going to say.

"Come on, don't keep us in suspense," said Dad. "I am eager to finish my roasted chicken."

"Chill, guys, it was superb," I said with a big smile on my face.

"Really?" said Dad, getting up from the chair and patting me on the back, as if I had won some gold trophy.

"Come on Dad, don't make an issue," I said, feeling bashful. "I just went out for lunch, not a big deal."

"Come on, Bessie," Mom said, picking a piece of chicken with a fork, "It is a big deal for us. You hardly come out of your room." I nodded my head, mixing rice with pulse.

"In front of Tiya, I am just a plain Jane," I said.

"Don't compare yourself with others," said Mom. "Be comfortable in your skin."

"You are right Mom," I said smiling.

"I felt very much at ease in my black shorts and Barbie Tee." All of us finished our meals, chit-chatting about general stuff - Dad about his upcoming projects, Mom about her friends, and I, about the recent books I had finished reading.

IN MY ROOM

As soon as I placed my head on the soft pillow, I heard a chirp-twitter.

"Hey Birdie," I got up, excited.

"Where are you? I know you are hiding in my room somewhere."

Woosh! Birdie fluttered in front of me.

"Birdie, I can see you are very inquisitive to know about my day out," I said. "Am I right?"

"I can tell from your face, that it went super-duper fantabulous."

"Oh yes!" I yelled out, squishing my squish mallow, which Pinky had gifted me on Friendship Day.

"The credit goes to you, Birdie."

"Bessie, I just showed you the path. After all, it is you who put the effort to walk on it," replied Birdie.

"Come on, stop being so modest," I said lying on my stomach. "Do you know that for the first time, I was comfortable talking to a stranger?" While I was saying this, I could feel my eyes twinkling like stars. I was not anxious at all.

"Birdie, I was so confident."

"Great," Birdie replied. "I am so happy for you, I always knew, Bessie, that you can do it."

"Tiya was looking great in her bottle green dress and white sandals. Initially, I had felt a little bit conscious of myself, thinking that I was in shorts and a Barbie tee, but then your magical words made me move forward- 'Be who you are'."

"Oh, Bessie, I am extremely proud of you," said Birdie, fluttering its vibrant wings.

"Guess what, Birdie?" I said, talking non-stop. "Tiya was asking me about novels and authors. She has just started reading. She was surprised to know that I had so much knowledge about books and authors."

"Bessie, that's why you should never think yourself inferior to others. Just remember, no one can insult you without your permission. Always think highly of yourself. Give importance to yourself, and value your work, only then your friends will value you," said Birdie.

"Birdie, I promise, I will always heed your words. Will you promise me something?"

"Tell me," chirped Birdie, perched on my bean bag.

"Please don't ever leave me. Pinky and you are my best friends," I said.

"Bessie, don't worry, I am always here. Think of the present, don't spoil the present worrying about the future," said Birdie.

"If you make your present beautiful, the future will take care of itself."

"Such meaningful words Birdie," I said, clasping my book.

"I promise I will never complain."

"Awesome!" chirped Birdie. "Okay, lately what have you purchased?"

"A few weeks back I had shopped with Pinky, but I didn't feel like buying anything, except for a few books," I said, showing her the books I had purchased.

"That's what I wanted to hear Bessie," chirped Birdie, getting down from the bean bag.

"Can you make it clear?" I said, confused. Sometimes it was difficult to understand Birdie.

"Bessie, it's simple," said Birdie. "You didn't buy clothes and other stuff because you didn't need them. If you had bought more than you needed, then you would have wasted your parents' money. Why hoard things uselessly, isn't it?"

"Birdie, I never thought of it that way," I said with a grimace.

"Bessie, right now you are quite young to understand what I am saying," said Birdie, "But always keep in mind what I have just said. Material things don't give you happiness, they give only misery."

"Oh Birdie, what you are saying now is flying over my head," I said beaming. "Maybe when the time is right, I will remember your words. But one thing is for sure, buying things always makes me happy."

"Yes, very true dear," said Birdie. "That is with everyone. People think material things give them happiness, but it's just temporary happiness."

"Whew, Birdie," I gasped. "Can you explain with examples?"

"Fine," chirped Birdie. "Just think that you are sad and have thought of treating yourself by buying a pair of jeans."

"Okay," I nodded my head, imagining myself buying jeans which I had been eyeing for few days. Birdie continued, "You bought that pair of jeans with your pocket money and unknowingly it got stuck on the door and tore."

"OMG!" I gasped.

"I cannot imagine my new clothes getting torn."

"Just a little while ago that pair of jeans was giving you happiness, and now the same jeans are giving you sadness. Now what do you have to say, Bessie?"

I didn't have any answer for that. I was too confused. Tears were coursing down, thinking of the torn jeans.

"Bessie," chirped Birdie, hopping on my bed. "My intention was not to make you cry, but to make you understand the true meaning of happiness."

"What is happiness, then?" I asked, still tears on my face.

"Bessie, it's very difficult to understand its true meaning," said Birdie. "In simple terms, happiness means contentment. Be happy with what you have. Appreciate the things you have. Be grateful that you can sleep in such a beautiful soft bed. Your parents can afford to send you to a nice school. You get to eat delicious food every day. You have nice clothes to wear. You have different toys to play with. You have eyes with which you can read so many books. Above all, you have wonderful parents who can look after you. There are so many people who are under-privileged compared to you, who would love to be in your place."

I just sat there, motionless. Birdie was right, I thought. I was lucky.

"Birdie," I said very quietly. "I have you and Pinky as well."

"Bessie, don't worry," chirped Birdie, "I am not telling you to not purchase the things you love, shop and live your life, laugh aloud, sing along, eat, have fun, be happy, but just maintain balance in your life, and don't spend your life complaining."

"Thank you, Birdie, I will keep in mind whatever you have said," I said, blowing her a kiss.

6:00 PM

Yippeee! I danced around the room. I opened the window wide and let the crispy wind blow in.

Saisa and Maggie were looking at me, wondering what happened to me. I was in total bliss because eventually, my exams were over. No exams mean holidays!

Just then, my door opened, and barged in my bestie, Pinky. She was also looking very jubilant.

"Hi Bessie," Pinky squeaked, jumping. We held our hands like little girls and danced in circles like we used to do when we were in kindergarten. We got queasy after some time, so we stopped and flopped on the floor, gasping.

"Wow, it was fun Bess," said Pinky.

"Hey, after ages you have called me by my short name," I said smilingly.

"Yes, I do that when I am on top of the moon," Pinky said grinning.

My dad entered the room with a big smile on his face.

"So, girls, all set for camping tomorrow?"

"Dad," I said. "It's just for one night, not a whole month," I said, grinning.

"Still, you have to get your necessary things ready," said Dad. I looked at Pinky and we thought he was right.

"Wait for secrets tomorrow," I said. I knew Pinky hated secrets.

"Come on, Bessie, you know I hate secrets. Please tell me no."

"No way," I said, "I will tell you tomorrow while camping, did you forget what you did to me during the slumber party?"

"Hey, you still haven't forgiven me?" asked Pinky, a little worried.

"Hey, hey, relax," I said. "Nothing like that, I was just kidding." Pinky was almost in tears. I didn't want to ruin the holiday mood.

9:30 PM

IN MY ROOM

"Birdie, Birdie," I called out. "I want to talk to you."

"Princess called me, and I am here," twittered Birdie, as usual appearing out of nowhere.

"OMG! Someday, surely, you'll give me a heart attack," I said, gasping.

"Birdie, we are all set for our little camp tomorrow."

"Marvellous!" said Birdie, fluttering its wings.

"I am thrilled to see your face glowing."

"Yes, Birdie, you are right. I am on cloud nine," I said hugging Maggie.

"It's become possible because of you."

"Give a pat on your shoulder, Bessie," said Birdie, hopping on my bed.

"You decided to change yourself and remain blissful, that's why you are in this situation. It's just a matter of choice."

"You are always modest, Birdie," I said, smiling.

"I used to always stay gloomy in my room. You taught me to smile. You taught me to live a life. Will you join me in the camp? I would love you to meet Pinky."

"To be honest, this is a moment for both of you," said Birdie. "Don't worry about me, I'll be watching over you all the time."

"Birdie, this is the first time I am camping, even though it is for a night," I said. "You know very well that I never leave my bed."

"Every time is the first time, Bessie," said Birdie. "Just explore things. Life is an adventure."

"What would I do if a problem crops up? Whom should I call?" I asked.

"Hey Bessie, don't panic," said Birdie, perched on top of my Harry Potter book. "Just close your eyes, and call out for me, I'll be there."

"Promise?" I asked.

"Yes," said Birdie. "But you'll have so much fun that you won't have time to call out for me."

"Come on, Birdie," I said, eyes brimming with tears. "You are always close to my heart." Birdie flew away and I took out Enid Blyton's Famous Five books and started reading them.

6:00 PM

HURRAY! CAMP TIME

Our dads (Pinky's and mine), helped us set up the tent, whereas our moms were busy preparing snacks as if we were going to camp not for a night, but for days.

Pinky had a small eight-year-old sneaky brother named Winnie. He was extremely cute, fair, and chubby. No one could beat him for his naughtiness. Pinky always tried her best to keep him out of sight when we were together. Guys, you must be wondering why I am raising the issue of Winnie suddenly. He, the little monster, insisted that he would join us for the camping. Pinky gave him such a horrifying stare (NO YOU CANNOT COME). The poor guy fled, calling out for his mom. We went inside the tent. I had a 'wow' kind of feeling. No wonder people always craved for camping. Our plush pillow was there. Small lanterns were kept. The tent was looking extremely cozy. A heavy mattress was laid. Three cheers to our parents. Thanks, Dad, I whispered, beaming.

"Happy?" asked Dad. "Super-duper," I replied jumping. I know this will be my best camp.

"Girls," called out my mom. "Get your things ready."

Our parents were planning to have their quiet supper. Well and good. I felt bad for Winnie. I decided to lend him my video game. "It must be returned in one piece, okay?" I warned Winnie.

"Promise," said Winnie, snatching the video game and starting to play.

8:00 PM

"Wow, Pinky. We have decorated our tent very well," I said, admiring our mini tent. We had placed small electric starry lights. It was looking awesome. "Whose idea was it, after all?" said Pinky, smirking.

"Come on, stop blowing your own trumpet," I teased her. Though this was my first time, Pinky had gone camping with her parents ample of times. Sometimes I wonder how we became besties. She is an extrovert whereas I am....Before I could complete my thought, Pinky waved the book she was reading in front of me. "Again lost in thoughts? What are you thinking about? Anything interesting?"

"Nothing," I said. "I was missing my bed. I have never left my room all these years, so I was feeling a little uncomfortable. Hope you don't mind what I just said."

"Hey take a chill pill," said Pinky, sprawling. "You'll enjoy it, trust me."

"What are we going to do the whole night?" I asked. "Don't know what made me ask this stupid question."

Pinky didn't answer for a while, and she suddenly started guffawing loudly. "What happened, silly?" I asked confused.

"Bessie, I am very sure God must have been in His worse mood when he created you," Pinky said, still laughing. Seeing Pinky laugh, I couldn't help myself from laughing. Just then, my phone rang. It was my mom, asking if we needed anything. Pinky snatched the phone and said, "Don't worry about us aunty, we will let you know if we need anything."

10:00 PM

MY EXPERIENCE IN A CAMP

How time elapsed, I didn't even realize. Eventually, I settled down grumbling and nagging Pinky, about how I missed my dolls and books in my room. She consoled me by saying, "Relax, Bessie, it'll be a memorable night for you." Pinky aggravated me more by showing her long vampire-like nails with multi-coloured nail polishes. I was supposed to say 'awesome' but blurted out 'awful' instead. What are friends for, if you cannot be honest, aren't it readers?

"I knew you wouldn't be impressed," Pinky said, sniggering.

"Obviously," I nodded. "It looks so scary."

"These are fake ones, you silly," said Pinky, taking out nails, one by one.

"Oh really?" I asked, amazed. "Wow, they look so real."

"Don't know which world you live in," Pinky said, stashing those terrifying nails in her box.

"I live on this earth, right where you live," I said, a bit annoyed.

"Chill, someone looks irritated," teased Pinky, hitting me with a squish mallow.

"Come on, don't be serious, I was just pulling your leg."

"It's okay," I said, giving her a big wide smile. But my smile didn't last long.

"Pinky, Pinky," I stammered, "Something is..."

"What's wrong?" Pinky asked. "Speak..."

"A big spider is crawling on your tee...!"

"A spider?" said Pinky. "Where? Idiot, why are you staying still? Pass me the insect spray! Do hurry up."

I could see her face turning pasty out of fear. Thank goodness, I found it on time. She grabbed it from me. She must have finished half the bottle, spraying on the huge black, hairy spider.

"Whew! That was scary," I gasped. "Do you still say camping is fun?"

"Obviously," Pinky said, taking a deep breath.

"These incidents will be cherished throughout our lives, trust me."

"You talk like an old granny, with spectacles perched at the tip of the nose," I teased her.

"Comparatively yes, I am much wiser," she said pinching my nose.

Gradually, I started enjoying the night. It was not bad after all, I thought.

"Shall we go out of the tent for a while?" asked Pinky. "I am feeling stuffy, don't know why."

"Maybe due to that spray," I said, suddenly remembering the huge spider.

"Oh yes," said Pinky. "We should have come out, there and then. What idiots we are?"

So, we came out of the tent and took in some crispy fresh air.

"Let's flop on the bed and count the stars," said Pinky. "Believe me, it's real fun. Winnie and I often do this."

"Are you mad?" I asked, flopping on the grass, "Why would I do that? It's impossible to count the stars."

"Hey dumbo," said Pinky. "When you count the stars, you'll start noticing that there are different types of stars in the sky, although I am clueless about their names. Winnie and I love keeping funny names for them."

"Okay, let's try," I said, finding it interesting.

"Let me try it, then," We started counting the stars like small kids.

"Can you see the biggest star?" asked Pinky. I looked closely and guessed the star she must be pointing at, the one I was looking at. I nodded, "Yes."

"What should we name the star?" asked Pinky.

"Oh yes," I said, pretty excited, "What about 'Winking eyes'?" I asked.

"What made you say that?" asked Pinky, still gazing at the stars.

"Because when I looked at it, I felt as if it was winking at me," I said.

"See?" Pinky said. "Isn't naming stars fun?"

So, we sat outside for a while. We ended up naming Miss Charming for a small star. We decided to enter the tent finally because it was getting pretty chilly outside. Once we were inside the tent, we scrutinised the place very carefully, to check if there were any horrifying, hairy creatures crawling anywhere. Once we were sure there were none anywhere, we decided to put on the headlights and read for a while. I was reading Harry Potter and the Chamber of Secrets and Pinky was reading Maze Runner. This reading habit is common among us, otherwise we are poles apart.

"Hey," after some time, both of us said together, to each other. Then we closed the books and couldn't help laughing loudly.

"I am starved."

"I was going to say the same thing," said Pinky.

"Should we dive into chips?"

"I am always ready for chips," I said, hearing the words chips. We tore open two to three packets of Lay's chips and started gobbling.

"We are eating as if we had been famished for years," said Pinky, munching on chips. I agreed; chips are too tempting to resist. After finishing the chips, Pinky crushed the chips packet and put it in a plastic bag. Compared to me, she is very methodical.

"Pinky," I said, pretty seriously. "I must confess something to you."

"Confess?" said Pinky, getting up. "What?"

"It's okay. Will tell you later," I loved keeping her in suspense. I knew she hated this.

"Come on, you know very well I hate suspense," pleaded Pinky. "Tell me."

I kept silent for a while.

"Come on, Bessie," said Pinky, shaking me hard.

"Relax," I said, clearing my throat.

"Let's watch a horror movie. After that, I will surely tell you."

"I hate you for this," grumbled Pinky, hitting me with my Teddy.

"Hey, you are hurting my teddy," I screamed, snatching Maggie from her.

"Okay, then tell me," said Pinky, grabbing Maggie.

"I had kissed a guy when I was ten," I said, trying to control my laughter.

"Ha, ha, ah! What?" Pinky asked, laughing and rolling on the mat.

"Whom are you kidding? Do you think I will believe you?"

"Fine, believe it or not," I shrugged.

She looked into my eyes, wondering whether to believe me or not.

"Seriously?" Pinky asked. I nodded. I was crossing my fingers hard behind my back.

"Then why didn't you tell me?" asked Pinky, still confused.

"I am telling you now," I said, trying to be bold. "I tell you all my secrets and you have been holding this from me," said Pinky, looking a bit hurt. I didn't want to spoil her mood, so immediately I said, "Hey, take a chill pill. I kissed a boy but..."

"But what?" asked Pinky, a bit annoyed.

"In my dreams," I completed, laughing.

"Slowly you are showing me your true colors, huh?" Pinky said, hitting me with Maggie.

"Give my teddy back!" I yelled, "Before you rip her apart."

Both of us remained silent for a while. "I never knew camping with my best friend would be so fun," I said, giving Pinky a tight hug.

"I always told you to come out of your cocoon," said Pinky, smiling.

"I am happy that you are enjoying, Bessie. t"

"Who's going to finish this pizza?"

"We, who else?" I said, opening the two boxes of salami cheese pizza that Pinky's mom had prepared.

Both of us enjoyed our yummy pizza, talking of our childhood days, how Pinky had pushed me in the swimming pool, and I had not let her play with my dolls for days. Once, I had placed a banana peel, outside her bedroom door, she had slipped and had denied me from riding her bicycle for two weeks.

"Those were the days," said Pinky, taking the last piece of the pizza.

"How old were we?" I asked.

"Do you remember?"

"Obviously. We were six years old," said Pinky, tittering.

"I still remember what you were wearing, a pink lacy frock with blue ribbons." Both of us laughed till tears pelted down. I gave a glance at my watch. How time flies when you are happy, I mused.

"Pinky, it's already past 1:00 AM."

"A very good morning, dear," said Pinky, stretching her arms.

"I really want to watch a series, which is in trend right now on Netflix."

"Which one?" I asked, "Creeped out," Pinky said. "Have you watched?"

"Oh yes. I have watched one episode,"

"It's creepy. Let's go for it."

So, both of us are all set to watch, the T.V. series, 'Creeped Out'. Thank God I was not alone. By the time one episode was over, I had bitten all my nails out of fear. Pinky, on the other hand, gulped a whole bottle of lemonade.

"Whew, that was spine-chilling," said Pinky. "Are you ready to watch another one?"

"Oh yes," I said, pretty excited, though I was terrified from inside. We were halfway through the movie when it started raining. It was a drizzle at first, then gushing rain. Pinky switched off the laptop and dragged me outside the tent.

"Pinky, what are you doing?" I yelled. "I am going to get drenched."

"That's what I want," said Pinky. "Just believe me, you'll thank me later."

Pinky was so true. Dancing, jumping, and playing in the rain was so thrilling. I used to think that people who danced in the rain were fools, but now when I was dancing in the rain myself. I was an idiot then, not to know the importance of nature.

"Remember, I always called you, for rain dance," said Pinky, stretching her arms and jumping.

"Yes," I squealed. "I always closed my windows and curtains when it rained." Each drop that fell on my face, hands, and feet was doing wonders for me. I had not experienced this kind of bliss in life.

"Hey Bessie, too much mess is also not good. You should do everything in balance."

"It's Birdie," I squealed, looking here and there for her, but couldn't find her.

"Who's Birdie?" asked Pinky, looking confused.

I had forgotten that Birdie is my secret friend, and even Pinky didn't know about her.

"Chill, chill," I said, trying to make my face normal. "Just my imaginary friend."

"Phew! You and your imagination," said Pinky, getting inside the tent. She believed me easily because she knew that I often lived in the world of books.

"Pinky, thanks a ton," I said, embracing her. "I never knew dancing in the rain could be so exciting. For the first time, I thought I lived and not just survived."

"Wow, Miss Philosopher," clapped Pinky. "From where do you get these high and mighty words?? I told you, you would thank me for this."

"Now I am feeling really sleepy," I said, getting inside my Disney princess quilt.

"Me as well," said Pinky giving a big yawn. We were about to sleep when I suddenly got up.

"Hey Pinky, get up, what is that gift-wrapped box in the corner?" Pinky got up, rubbing her eyes, "Oh yes, I wonder, someone must have kept it," "Hey, do you think it could be a bomb?" I said, frightened. "Come on, that's why I tell you to not read too many mystery books," said Pinky.

"I will go and see."

"Na, don't go," I pulled her tee.

"Someone may be waiting outside, to see us open the box."

"Your imagination runs wild, Bessie," said Pinky. "You can be a great storyteller. Be positive sometimes, who knows, it might be a surprise gift from our parents."

"Oh, it can be. I never thought of that," I said, trying to smile. Both of us, headed gingerly to the box. It was wrapped in glittering blur paper. "Hey, something is written here," said Pinky, reading a small note.

"HAPPY CAMPING," SAID THE NOTE.

"It was not my parents' handwriting," Pinky without saying anything, started unwrapping the box. It was a wooden box. Both of us looked at each other. What could it be? I pondered. I missed Birdie. Wished I could call her. She would have given me the solution in a jiffy.

"Should we open it?" I asked, my hands trembling.

"I am warning you still, Pinky."

"We will open it," said Pinky.

"We will show them that we are not cowards," Pinky opened the box and popped out a laughing joker, attached to a spring, singing, "Fooled you!"- repeatedly. Aahh...!! Both of us fell backward.

"I had warned you, it was a kind of a trick," I said, my heart playing hopping and catching.

"But whoever did it, it was fun, right?" said Pinky, trying her best to sound bold." But I knew that underneath she was terrified.

"Hey, Pinky, wait, there is a small slip here," I said, trying to read what was written.

"What's written?" asked Pinky. It read, "A punishment for not letting me in your tent."

"Wait till I get hold of the little rascal," grunted Pinky, crinkling up the paper. It was Winnie, after all. Anyway, our camping ended with both sweet as well as sour experiences. I should rather say, that more than sour, it was sweet. What I noticed about Pinky was that she prayed before she went to sleep. I was clueless about what she said in prayers. I had never prayed in my life so didn't know what to ask God. I didn't want to disturb Pinky by asking her how to pray. I thought I would ask Birdie. She will give me the best possible answer. With these happy thoughts in my mind, I went off to sleep for the first time under my tent.

9:30 PM

IN MY ROOM

Birdie, as usual, was perched on her favorite place, my bookshelf, where I had kept all my new and old books. I couldn't help myself from admiring her beautiful colorful wings.

"It seemed you had a marvellous time Bessie," chirped Birdie.

"How did you know?" I asked, sprawled on my Barbie bedsheet.

"Everyone can tell seeing your face," said Birdie.

"You look fresh, energetic, full of life, and no more gloominess. I also noticed that you laugh a lot more these days."

"Birdie, you know very well that it's all because of you," I said. "I still have so many things to learn as I grow up."

"Like I told Bessie, if you hadn't taken the initiative, I would not have been able to do anything," said Birdie. Birdie was not hovering around my room this time. It just sat in one place, flapping its wings.

"I always believed you Birdie, don't know the reason why," I said.

"More than me, you believed in your capabilities," said Birdie, "Until and unless you believe in yourself, you would not have been able to believe others, Bessie."

"Yes, you are true," I nodded.

"Now tell me something Bessie, do you still get annoyed by the twitter of the birds?" asked Birdie.

"No way," I said. "I love the sound of the twittering of the tiny birds. I was a fool to close the windows when I heard the chirping of the birds; I couldn't stop myself from crying."

"Hey Bessie, no need to cry," said Birdie. "Realisation is the biggest asset. This is called experience. It's time for celebration. As you grow older, you'll have more beautiful experiences. Life will be a bundle of surprises. It will unfold itself in its course. Do not be scared. Face it with God in your heart." Then I remembered, I had to ask Birdie regarding 'prayers'.

"Birdie, I have to ask you something," I said. "Why do we pray? I had noticed Pinky praying before retiring herself to bed, don't know what she said while praying. I thought I would ask you."

"A very good question, Bessie," said Birdie, coming closer to me. Birdie had never come close to me like this. I could see every different color in her feathers.

"Prayer is heart-to-heart communication with God," said Birdie. "Can we talk with God?" I asked, confused.

"Of course! You can talk with God. God is everywhere. You can ask him for anything. But don't ask for the wrong things," said Birdie, still perched close to me.

"Can you make it clearer, please?" I requested.

"Suppose you haven't studied for your exam and you pray to God to make you pass with flying colors. Do you think God will listen to your prayer?" asked Birdie.

"God will see how devoted you are, and then only reward you accordingly."

"Birdie, I am still confused, regarding how to pray and what to say during prayers," I persisted.

"Fine," said Birdie, "You don't have to perform any rituals to pray. Just join your hands, close your eyes, think of God, and say whatever comes in your heart. The good things you have done during the day, the mistakes you've made, if by chance you have hurt anyone, if you want to say sorry, say sorry to Him. Tell Him your goals, wishes, what are your favorite dishes, which boy you like, and ask God to keep everyone blessed."

"Praying is very easy," I said, my eyes sparkling.

"It is like talking with you. I tell you everything, don't I?"

"Correct. You got me now," said Birdie.

"God is your best friend. Everyone can leave you, but He will never leave you."

"What other things can I talk about with God?" I asked, getting inquisitive.

"You can share with God your happiness, sadness, your problems, everything," said Birdie.

"But will God answer me, like you do?"

"Of course!" said Birdie. "These are called miracles Bessie, He answers through miracles."

Tears were continuously pelting down my face.

"I have understood everything now, Birdie. From now on, I will also start praying regularly. Will you come a bit closer? I want to whisper in your tiny ears," I said.

Birdie, for the first time, came very close to me, I whispered, "YOU ARE A MIRACLE TO ME, BIRDIE."

I noticed something sparkling on my pillow after Birdie flew away. I picked it up and to my utter surprise, it was a PINK FEATHER, which Birdie had left for me. I was very thrilled. In my entire life, I had never seen such a beautiful, glistening feather. It was radiating soft pinkish light and mellow fragrance. I took out my small, recently bought jewelry box, which I had bought, thinking of keeping something precious. I placed the 'feather' gently inside the box. It was continuously spreading fragrance, I said under my breath-

"BIRDIE, YOU ARE STILL THE ONE FOR ME."

ABOUT THE AUTHOR

"Fight For Your Fairytale."

Anju Pradhan, since childhood always lived in the world of imagination, magic and miracles. She always believed that every person has a little child within. The tiny child just needs to come out and explore the magical universe. Besides, magical world, the author believes that God is within us. The heart is the abode of God, so keep the conscience pure. That is all God asks from us. Universe is her home and all the people are her family.

www.ingramcontent.com/pod-product-compliance
Lightning Source LLC
LaVergne TN
LVHW041610070526
838199LV00052B/3072